In Full Uniform

Anthony Carnovale

iUniverse, Inc.
Bloomington

In Full Uniform

iUniverse books may be ordered through booksellers or by contacting:

iUniverse
1663 Liberty Drive
Bloomington, IN 47403
www.iuniverse.com
1-800-Authors (1-800-288-4677)

*Because of the dynamic nature of the Internet, any Web addresses or
links contained in this book may have changed since publication and
may no longer be valid. The views expressed in this work are solely those
of the author and do not necessarily reflect the views of the publisher,
and the publisher hereby disclaims any responsibility for them.*

ISBN: 978-1-4502-7101-1 (sc)
ISBN: 978-1-4502-7102-8 (ebook)

Printed in the United States of America

iUniverse rev. date: 11/22/2010

For Gregory

...he felt like a boy who knows nothing, but is about to know everything, and feels the same dark fear both of knowing and not knowing.

Elias Canetti, *Auto-da-Fe*

CHAPTER ONE

At the ripe old age of thirteen, Jesse Cullen was beginning to feel like an old man.

Instead of looking forward to going to school, hanging out with friends, and skateboarding until bedtime, he thought about his grandfather and how he would talk about the good old days as if the good old days were too far gone to be of any use at all.

"When I was your age . . . " he'd begin, but before he could finish the sentence, the old man would cry and say goodbye to another memory that could serve him no use. Nothing could keep him from growing old. Not even memories.

Jesse had also tried to avoid getting old, and he was only thirteen. Growing up was nothing like he had been promised.

The sky was now halfway between dark and light, and Jesse wished he were sleeping instead of looking out his bedroom window at five-thirty in the morning.

If there was one thing that he was sure of, it was what five-thirty in the morning looked like. At this early hour, things moved at a much slower pace than at any other time in Jesse's day. Streetlights shone brighter than the fading stars, and lonely cars tiptoed down the street. He watched one turn into some driveway that led to some house where a family was sleeping and some fortunate children still dreamed. For most, going to bed at night meant putting an end to the day; for Jesse, it meant the start of a whole new one.

Last night he dreamt that he was down by the pond behind the school, sitting on a rock, trying to cut his wrist with a knife. Everyone from school was in attendance: teachers, students, principals, vice-principals, even the custodians in their blue uniforms. There were friends and enemies, but Jesse had a hard time discerning one from the other. They stood three deep, cheering him on from the other side of the pond, reminding him of who he was and what he would always be:

"*LOO*-SER!"

"*LOO*-SER!"

"*LOO*-SER!"

They chanted in unison, in full uniform, never skipping a beat or missing a note. Jesse tried to keep pace with their taunts, pushing and pulling the knife across his naked wrist, anxiously waiting for blood to appear and for his life to end. The knife was too dull—Jesse's pain, however, was not.

Out of breath and overwhelmed with grief, Jesse fell to his knees, looked up into an empty sky, and cried. From across the pond, he heard the crowd booing and yelling.

"Try again until you get it right!"

"You can do it!"

"Don't give up!"

Their words of encouragement were followed by a tangle of jeers, cheers, and whistles, until they all fell back in synch and picked up where they had left off:

"*LOO*-SER!"

"*LOO*-SER!"

"*LOO*-SER!"

Jesse pressed his hands over his ears, but he could still hear them. Hoping to at least wipe the crowd from his sight, he closed his eyes and prayed that when he opened them they'd be gone. But when he did open his eyes, he could still see them and hear them. The crowd took more out of Jesse's life than the blade of the knife ever could.

He hung his head in shame over the lip of the pond, but the last thing he needed to see was his reflection in the water. He could see tears beginning to swell and he watched them trickle down his cheek, working their way through his acne as if his face was a slalom course. The sight of his own face sickened him. He stared at his reflection and wished he could simply do away with it.

"If I can kill my reflection, I might be able to kill myself," he surmised. He stabbed at the water with the knife, following through with the little life he had left. But Jesse's reflection, like everything and everyone in his life, would not disappear and leave him alone.

His reflection looked up at him and laughed. "You can't even kill yourself right, you fucking loser." He watched his face sink through the murky water and disappear.

And once again Jesse woke to the one word that put him to sleep each and every night, the same word he woke up to at five-thirty this morning: *Loser.* He had been called loser so often, in his dreams and at school, that there were times when Jesse had forgotten his own name.

Unable to fall back asleep, Jesse stood at his bedroom window looking out at all the houses that lined the street and at the sidewalks he traversed each day to get to school.

He could see the Hasty Market, the dollar store, the Pizza Depot, the cleaners, the Get-Well Centre, and the Chinese restaurant that was never busy. The trees looked out of place, and all the houses looked the same. It was a neighbourhood constructed out of straight lines and primary colours, filled with strip malls and megamalls, a gas station on every corner, and a mini-van in every driveway.

The neighbourhood looked to stretch out as far as the horizon. New things were being built before anything had a chance to grow old.

"If this shit keeps up, I may never get to be old!" Jesse muttered to himself. He thought about all the things he had heard about growing old when he used to feel young:

"I can't wait to be a grown up!"

"I can't wait to get my license!"

"I can't wait to be nineteen!"

"I can't wait . . . "

"I can't wait . . . "

"I *can* wait," Jesse declared to no one but himself.

The one thing grown-ups didn't tell kids about growing up was just how tough growing up really was.

He looked over the pointed rooftops of the neighbourhood houses until his gaze drifted to the vacant crucifix that stood atop St. Gregory's Elementary School. Jesse couldn't help but think of a headstone and how the school itself was like a coffin and that everything inside of it was dying because he was.

Beneath that cross were hallways and classrooms where all the kids that didn't look the same or sound the same or act the same—the kids who didn't fit in—were reminded of it every day.

Last week it was because his acid-wash jeans were "so whack," and his hair was "fagotty," and how his acne was "never going to go away—but I wish you would, man!"

"God, you look awful!"

Jesse fixed his eyes on the empty crucifix and thought about God and all the things that he hoped were true.

"I thought Jesus died for our sins," he said aloud, and hoped that he hadn't somehow committed a sin. He sighed, steaming up the window, and was suddenly reminded that he was alive—then he remembered his dream and wished he wasn't. He was only a month away from graduating, but wished it were tomorrow.

He took his eyes off the cross that marked his elementary school and looked over to the one that stood atop St. Elizabeth's Secondary School. He had a funny feeling that things might not change as much he hoped they would when he started high school in September.

Jesse was reminded of this just last week as he was hanging out with his best friend Ryan. Ryan's brother, Adam, told them about a lockdown that the principal of his high school initiated because there were rumours going around that someone had brought a gun to school. Adam laughed his way through the entire story.

"It was so awesome! It was just like in the movies!"

Jesse was smart enough to know that life wasn't a movie; movies ended after a couple of hours—the drama in Jesse's life was heading into its thirteenth year.

His reflection, like a ghost, stared back at him through the window. It had been a while since he had looked at himself, so he was surprised that he stood there and looked at his green eyes, his unkempt hair, his ears, his nose, his chin. He had his grandfather's lips and his mother's teeth. He was thirteen years old and tall for his age.

Over the past few months he could feel his body stretching and thought at times he had even heard his bones cracking. He knew it wasn't possible, but one day was convinced that he had heard something go pop in his knee.

Bones cracking, voice squeaking, skin breaking out.

The part that he liked least about growing up was the acne, because it was all the kids at school seemingly paid any attention to, as if the rest of his face or body or very existence simply didn't matter. When they called him names and made fun of him and cheered him towards death in his dream, they were looking at his acne. They never looked him in the eye.

With his own eyes, he looked at his reflection in the window and reached out to wipe the tear that was working its way through his acne down his cheek, but his thumb met his thumb, and he couldn't stop himself from crying.

"This is why I don't like looking at myself!"

He had developed a habit of avoiding all mirrors and objects that gave off a reflection. This was by no means an easy task in a teenager's life, when a mirror often serves as a best friend, a confidant, a reminder that people existed and that they looked okay (or of what they needed to fix so that they would).

To Jesse, looking in the mirror only reminded him of what they called him each and every day:

Pizza face
Connect-the-Dots
Pepperoni face
Nasty

And when they couldn't think of anything else, there was always the one word that summed things up best:

Loser.

Jesse ignored his reflection, and looked out at a world that was about to wake up.

The sun began to ascend at the horizon, and in a blink his reflection was only a shadow of its former self. Lights turned on and streets lights turned off as the stars looked forward to calling it a night. The world was waking and Jesse suddenly felt anxious; he couldn't let his mother see that he was up.

The thought of his mother cheered him briefly, but the thought of lying to her again wiped the smile from his face. He turned his back on himself and jumped into bed, feeling more tired this morning than he did when he went to bed last night.

It was the same routine day in and day out. Jesse was tired before his day even began, so he did the only thing that made him feel any better: he convinced himself that things would work out, that the bullying would stop, and that he would finally be able to feel and act his own age. Jesse thought about going back to sleep, but didn't think it was a particularly good idea—this time he might have a sharper knife.

Jesse lay in his bed and was glad to be away from the window and his reflection.

He wrapped himself in his grandmother's quilt, wishing it were her arms instead of a blanket that he had outgrown many years ago. He looked up at the toy plane that hung above his head from the ceiling.

He had always loved planes and hoped one day to fly one.

As a child he would run through parks and streets and living rooms with his arms outstretched, pretending he was up in the air with the birds and the clouds, gliding, coasting, and floating—the closest thing to an angel. When he was too old to believe in angels and realized that what he thought were angels were really planes that people had to fly, Jesse asked his father if he could be a pilot, because being off the ground and flying around free always seemed like a wonderful thing to be able to do.

His mother bought the toy plane because he had had a good first day at school. Jesse turned over onto his side and looked across his room at a mirror that he had plastered with pictures because he didn't want to run the risk of seeing himself. He settled his eyes on the picture that his mother had taken after his first day of school.

He had been looking for her the moment the bus turned the corner of his street. When he finally saw her, Jesse jumped up onto the seat and waved frantically. He yelled out to her and tried to push his hand through a window that was barely open.

"Mommy! Mommy!"

He was too excited to hear the bus driver tell him to sit down.

When his mother saw him get up from the seat, she followed his blonde hair to the front of the bus. She pulled a camera out of her pocket and snapped a picture the moment his foot hit the ground.

He was smiling, wearing a *Ghostbusters* T-shirt and the sweater his mother had given him just in case he got cold. The sweater was unzipped, and his stomach bulged over the pants that he was already starting to grow out of. His *Transformers* lunchbox was in his right hand and he was reaching out for her with his left. He missed her and couldn't wait to touch her.

"Say cheese, baby!"

"Cheeeese!"

Martin Paynesworth, Jesse's new friend and classmate, turned to his mother and sulked. "Mommy, how come you didn't take a picture of me?"

Martin's mother tugged her son's sweater in embarrassment and dragged him away, while Jesse and his mom walked and talked about all his new friends and the things he learned that day.

Later that evening, Jesse's parents took him to Wal-Mart and returned with the picture that he was now looking at and the plane that hung from his ceiling. When his father finished hanging it, his mother decided to toast the affair: "A gift, for my little Gift!"

Jesse drank his glass of milk and smiled up at his mother with a white moustache.

"Look at my old man," she laughed as she took the glass from Jesse and got him ready for bed.

He had to go to school tomorrow; something Jesse was hoping he didn't have to do today.

"Some gift," he thought.

He used to like it when she called him Gift. When he was younger the name had a wonderful ring to it. But at Erin Smyth's birthday party in grade three, Rudy Sinclair, a classmate of Jesse's, overheard Jesse's mom calling him Gift, and the next day at school they were making fun of him for of it.

"You think you're so special because your mommy calls you Gift? My mom calls me *Stupid*!"

Jesse was old enough to know that Gift was better than Stupid, but he didn't like being made fun of and spoke about it with his mother.

"Ma, why do you call me Gift? People at school say its stupid."

"They're just jealous, baby! I call you Gift because that's what you were and that's what you are: a gift."

She told Jesse that she had been pregnant twice before she had given birth to him. She told him what a miscarriage was and that the second one had occurred a day after Mother's Day, just over a year and a half before Jesse was born. "When the doctor told me that I would be carrying you to term, I almost punched him in the face. I thought he was lying! For a while, it was the happiest day of my life."

Jesse looked at her and wondered what had trumped his conception as the best day of his mother's life.

"Don't worry, honey! The happiest day was the day you were born. You were, and are, my gift from God. My little miracle. Now do you understand why I call you Gift?"

Jesse did; he was just grateful that she hadn't nicknamed him *Miracle*. "Can you at least stop calling me that when my friends are around?"

"My baby is in grade three and you're already worried about what people are saying to you. Try not to let it bother you." She wanted to tell him that he would have plenty of time to worry about things when he got older, but held her tongue and leaned over to give her little gift a kiss.

Jesse surveyed the other pictures. He could see the one of him and his dad fishing when he was six. There was the one of him and his cousins, Justin and Terry, at the air show. Jesse was supposed to be looking into the camera, but he loved planes more than his cousins did, so the camera had to settle for his smiling profile.

The pictures reminded him of his own "good old days": his first day of school, his first air show. There were pictures from picnics; pictures of him on his skateboard; pictures of him swimming and diving; and a picture of him as a baby, naked in the tub, feeling no sense of the shame then that he was feeling now as he looked at it.

He was smiling in every photo.

It was the smile that his friends and family complimented him on. They said he could light up a room with that smile. Jesse was reminded of why he had covered the mirror— pictures lied, the mirror didn't.

Tired, Jesse tried to forget about school as he waited for his mother to walk into his room and greet him with the same words she had used every morning since his first day of school:

CHAPTER TWO

"Good morning, my little gift. Time for you first day of school!"

Jesse squirmed in his sheets and brought his hands up to his eyes. "Mommy, I don't wanna go to school today." He turned his back on his mother and brought his blanket close to his chest, as if to anchor himself to his bed so he couldn't get up and go.

His mother sat down at the edge of the bed and ran her fingers through his hair. She reached for his arm and turned him around so that she could look her Gift in the eyes.

"Look at me."

Jesse sensed the sincerity in her voice, and looked at his mother.

"You have to go school, Jesse! You're going to make lots of new friends and learn so much!"

"But, I don't wanna learn new things, Mommy! I wanna stay here with you."

"Baby, I promise you're going to like it!"

Jesse, at five, understood the value of a mother's promise, and settled down and took her for her word.

"Can you come though, Mommy?"

"No, I can't come, but I will take you to the bus stop and I'll be there when you come back."

"But why do I haf'ta go to school?"

She took a few seconds to mull over his question, and tried to figure out the best way to tell him that today, his first day of school, was in many ways the first day of the rest of his life. "Remember how you said you wanted to go up in the air and fly with angels?"

He nodded.

"Well, if you want to go up into the air, you have to go to school."

Jesse let go of her hand and sat up and waited for her to dress him.

Later, while packing his grapes and cookies and filling his thermos with milk for his first day of school, Mary realized how quickly she had gone from breastfeeding her baby to making her little man a snack for school. She wiped away a tear and cursed herself for being so convincing.

Jesse was a good child who liked to sleep, eat, and laugh. He was full of energy and was rarely seen without something in his mouth. He had a curious nature and liked to touch everything. He had an outfit for every day of the month, and he liked to have his picture taken. He liked attention and his mother and father liked giving it to him. He was showered with toys and books and blankets and horse rides on knees and walks down to the pond to feed the ducks where he liked to point at all the planes that flew by. Sometimes he looked up at an empty sky and pointed at things his parents couldn't see.

"He's just like my Aunt Clara," Jesse's father, Joe, declared one day.

Mary looked at her husband, offended that the father of her little boy would compare her Gift to a woman that was clearly insane. "Honey, your Aunt Clara is freakin' nuts. She says she's pointing at all the angels!"

"Well, maybe they are *seeing* angels."

Mary looked down at her son and then up to the sky and smiled. All of a sudden, seeing angels didn't seem all that nuts.

Mary grabbed a napkin and, even though he couldn't read, she wrote her son a note because she had been thinking about this day for a long time. *Have a good day, Baby! Mommy and Daddy love you very much.*

She did her best to draw a plane to remind him why he and his mommy couldn't be together forever. She folded the napkin and shut the lunchbox, and reminded herself to tell him to keep the napkin and bring it home, so that she could put it into her *Book of Firsts.*

She bought the book day after she found out that she was pregnant for the first time and put it away when she miscarried for the second. At one point she thought about throwing it away, but felt as if she was somehow betraying herself. "I might get lucky!" she declared, because luck was the only thing that she had left.

There were plenty of pages in the book; lots of firsts that her first and only child would go through and she wanted to remember every single one of them. She collected his first fallen tooth, a piece of hair from his first haircut, and recorded his first word: *'mommy.* When she heard him speak it, she grabbed a pencil and, with Jesse's tiny hand inside her own, recorded his first word in his *Book of Firsts.* Today she would take a picture of his first day of school.

She walked back into the living room and looked at her nervous son. "Mommy is so proud of you Jesse! I want you to behave yourself at school today, okay? And if you're good, I'll buy you a toy tonight!"

She cupped his cheek with the palm of her hand, felt his warm skin, and leaned in to kiss him. "Let's go. You don't want to miss the bus on the first day, do you?"

He didn't have time to answer.

As he lay in bed, looking up at the plane, Jesse remembered his early school years as wonderful and fun. He was allowed to colour outside of the lines, making the sky green and the grass blue, and he was allowed to see things that weren't really there without being called crazy or retarded. Back then, schooldays were spent playing games and hearing stories and eating cookies and going for naps surrounded by your new best friends.

Jesse remembered the feeling that overcame him when he walked into a world full of colours and cardboard and construction paper, glue, books, desks, pillows, and the blackboard where Mrs. Simmons wrote the numbers one through ten and the alphabet in big block letters. They ate their snacks in a circle and napped until it was time for recess.

The kindergarten kids had their own playground with all the fixings: slides, plastic cars, monkey bars, swings, a sandbox, and an iron fence that kept them separated from the rest of the school. They ran, skipped rope, jumped and fell, slid down slides, and played hide-and-seek, despite the fact that there was no real place to hide. It was hide-and-seek that Jesse missed the most—it was so much easier to hide when he was a kid.

When the kids were tired from all the running and needed to catch their breath, some of them, including Jesse, would lean with their faces against the fence and watch the other kids, the older kids, run and play freely on the other side of the fence, free from adult supervision. After a while, that fence began to feel like a barrier to another world, and some of the kids would spend their entire recess looking out at the older kids. A secret desire would stir in some—they wanted to grow up as fast as they could so they could be on the other side, to do whatever it was older kids did.

Most were too busy playing tag to notice the few older kids, wishing *they* were on the other side of the fence playing tag and hanging from the monkey bars. It was only when a teacher yelled at them to go play with kids their own age that they turned their back on the younger ones and went and found a safe place to hide.

When the day ended to the sound of the bell, the kindergarten students gathered up their belongings and headed for the bus, waiting anxiously to see their parents and give them the new craft they had made that day.

On his first day, Jesse painted a picture that looked nothing like a plane flying through the air. It was perfect, because his mother told him so, and she hung it on the fridge where it stayed forever.

Jesse was doing fine at school. His teacher, Miss Simmons, was fond of him and sent personal letters home telling his parents what a good student he was. He was helpful and, unlike the rest of the kids, didn't seem to mind cleaning up the mess that he made painting pictures and cutting out snowflakes.

He may have been good, but he was far from perfect.

One day, Martin Paynesworth pushed Jesse to the ground because Jesse didn't want to give up his spot in line for the monkey bars. He cried and Martin was sent to the office. Miss Simmons held Jesse in her arms and brought him inside. She was patting the nape of his neck when Jesse lifted his head off her shoulder and noticed something red behind her. If he could have read it, he would have seen: Pull In Case of Fire. But the bright colour and the fact that it was within reach were all the instructions he needed.

The kids were excited—their jaws dropped at the sight of the big red truck that so many of them had played with at home. The only person who wasn't amused was Principal Edwards, since the school was on the hook for a big fine.

He called Jesse's mother and asked her to attend a meeting.

It was the first time the school had ever called Jesse's mother, and years later she would wish that it had been the last. She left work immediately and rushed off to see her son, less worried about a speeding ticket than about the well-being of her little Gift.

Jesse didn't remember the meeting, but his mother told him he had just sat there and pointed at the poster with all the airplanes.

After the excitement had subsided, Jesse settled into the routine of school and no longer fussed about having to go. But the only thing that changed quicker than the time was school; eventually, there was nothing elementary about elementary school for Jesse.

Junior and senior kindergarten were soon forgotten. All the younger kids who used to look out at the older kids through the fence were now on the other side of it, looking into the playground they once couldn't wait to grow out of. They wished they could go back to being a kid again. There was something about being on the other side of that fence that made everyone act differently. It seemed the bigger the world got, the more problems Jesse had.

To the seniors, going into grade one meant moving up into a bigger world, a graduation of sorts, where they were freed from the confines of the fence and were allowed access to other parts of a very big school and playground. But what the seniors didn't count on was the fact that they were going to be juniors once again—back on the bottom, waiting to be on top, and already looking forward to grade two.

Friends were no longer friends and they told each other so every day. Fred hated John because he wouldn't trade his Twinkie for a banana, Shirley hated Sandra because she wore the same shirt to school as her and made her look "retarded."

By the next week they were friends and found someone else to not like.

The school population was scattered throughout the playground and divided by grades, gender, nationalities, and style. The grade-ones were on the hill, while the grade-threes played Four-square, the grade five boys played soccer, while the girls in grade four jumped and screamed from the sidelines because Dustin scored a goal and Daniel had smiled at them. Jesse liked playing five rocks with Sukhi and handball with Mario, until Mario got tired of losing and didn't want to be Jesse's friend anymore.

It looked to Jesse like the only kids who didn't seem to be having any fun were the kids in grade six, seven, and eight. They always kept away from the smaller kids (unless they were chasing them) and walked around, never talking, wearing baggy clothes that made them look skinny and sick. But it wasn't so much they way they looked or the way they spit, fought, kicked, screamed, and yelled; it was the way they spoke. They used words kids weren't supposed to use. His mother told him so, as did the teachers, but the older kids didn't seem to mind.

All of a sudden getting older didn't look very appealing to Jesse, so he went on acting his age until it became a problem for a young person to act his age—which didn't take long.

The new curriculum implemented by the government was wreaking havoc on students and teachers alike. Jesse had something for homework almost every night. There was no more finger-painting, naps, snacks, or monkey bars. He had to memorize numbers and copy out sentences dozens of times until his cursive writing improved and he no longer wrote through the lines.

He was having a tough time with math. Mr. Embleton was growing increasingly concerned and invited Jesse's mother for a parent-teacher interview.

Mr. Embleton complained that Jesse was restless in class and had problems staying focused.

"Isn't there something you can change about the way you deliver the material?" Jesse's mother asked. "I remember when I was in school—"

"Mrs. Cullen," he interrupted, "let me assure you that it has nothing to do with the way the material is delivered."

Jesse sat quietly.

Jesse didn't struggle as much in his other classes. French was okay and English was fun, but math and science he simply didn't get. It was like the teacher was speaking in a foreign language, so he just doodled his way through the class and thought funny things and sometimes laughed out loud.

Jesse's marks continued to fall, so Mary spoke to Mr. Kearney, the guidance Counselor at St. Gregory's. Mr. Kearney recommended that Jesse see his family doctor and be tested for Attention Deficit Disorder.

Mary had heard about ADD on the radio and saw the commercials for Ritalin while watching television with Jesse after school. She acknowledged that Jesse did have a tendency to be rambunctious and hyper, but kids were supposed to be.

Mr. Kearney told her that there were other students in the class having the same problems. He couldn't tell her their names, but he assured her that Ritalin was an effective way of dealing with a child who could not sit still through a class.

Suddenly it dawned on Jesse who those kids were. "They're the kids that have to leave class, mama! They get made fun of all the time! I don't wanna be one of them!"

But when Mr. Kearney warned her that if they didn't get it treated quickly Jesse might suffer for it later on, she began to give the matter serious attention.

She talked it over with her husband that night over dinner.

"Mary, I was the same way when I was his age. We just need to be tougher on him, is all."

She looked at her beautiful Gift running around the living room, pretending he was a plane, flying away, running in circles, and jumping on the furniture. She decided that if he was ever going to get to fly a real plane that he'd have to do well in school and stay focused. She made an appointment with Dr. Sheffield for the following Monday.

The process was harder than she had expected. There were CAT scans, blood tests, questionnaires, and appointments— all because Jesse wasn't doing well in math and science. When it was all said and done and the prescription was filled, Jesse was on Ritalin. It didn't take long for him to settle down.

One night, a week after he began taking the medication, Mary watched Jesse on the kitchen chair sitting completely still and silent. "Joe, I'm not used to seeing him sit there and not move. He's not moving!"

"If the doctor says it's good for him, Mary, leave it be. Look at him: he's quiet, he's behaved—he's doing all the things that we couldn't get him to do ourselves. It's every parent's dream." He laughed, trying to get his wife to smile.

She didn't. "I'm calling the doctor!"

Dr. Sheffield told her that Jesse's body was reacting to the drug and it would take a while before he would get used to the foreign substance. He recommended that she speak to some of the parents at Jesse's school. She did.

Mary learned that many of the other parents had initially felt the same way, but when their children were no longer yelling and screaming and they could finally hear themselves think, they decided it was a good idea and even recommended it to family and friends. One mother suggested that Ritalin was "the best babysitter on the market."

Once the drug became a part of his daily routine (it usually followed brushing his teeth and combing his hair), Jesse no longer daydreamed or laughed out loud in class, but his grades didn't improve. It was decided that he be allowed to complete his class work in the resource room with teachers who were trained to work with students who couldn't pay attention in a typical classroom environment. Jesse was now one of the kids that he so desperately did not want to be.

When it was time for Jesse to leave his class and head to resource, he could hear some of his classmates snickering beneath their breath.

"He's a Special-Ed head!"

"He's retarded."

These were his friends from kindergarten: Martin, Rudy, Paul, Sean, and Jamal. The kids he used to play hide-and-seek with were now laughing at him, not with him.

After being tripped one day on his way down the aisle of desks, Jesse asked his mother why he was being made fun of.

"They're just jealous of the attention you're getting son. It is called Attention Deficit Disorder, isn't it?"

Jesse didn't get the joke. But he was beginning to get the jokes at school that were never really funny.

They called him stupid, idiot, and sometimes stupid.

They started using words he had never heard before, but understood nonetheless, for they were spit with such spite that he didn't need a dictionary to know what they were trying to say.

They were telling him that he wasn't cool enough, that he wasn't like anybody else and he never would be. It went from inside the class, to outside in the yard, to back inside the halls where they laughed and pointed and jeered and cursed him from behind their lockers.

In grade five, they stepped out from behind their lockers with new-found confidence and turned the mockery into a performance. The audiences loved it, for they were the ones who were not brave enough to say things on their own.

First it was the Ritalin, then it was the way he walked, the way he talked, the way he looked, the way he ran, and the way he cried all the way to the office so that he could call his mother at work to come pick him up.

Sometimes they'd throw things like sticks and stones and tell him to fetch because he was a dog who had a face only a mother could love.

In grade six, sticks and stones never broke any of Jesse's bones, but names really, really hurt him.

His classmates called him asshole, fuck-face, puke-face and shit-face. Jesse didn't know what it was about his face that attracted so much attention, but he hoped that it would stop.

He tried to remember the wonderful things his mother called him, but he spent more time at school than he did at home. And the truth was that at school, mothers didn't count.

"Hey, you have every right to be ugly—just don't abuse the privilege!"

"Nice face. Want a gun?"

When his best friends, Elly and Ryan, were away, Jesse hung out in the library and flipped through books with pictures of airplanes and magazines with pictures of perfect faces.

Mary had confronted the school on a number of different occasions, comforted by promises to take action but frustrated because nothing was ever done. She was told that it would play itself out, that it was just a phase and that the kids would grow out of it. Principal Edwards reminded her that Jesse wasn't the only one going through this sort of thing. She couldn't believe what she was hearing.

"I'm not worried about those kids! I'm worried about my son," she shot back. Her worry fell upon deaf ears, and the bullying continued.

When he wasn't being picked on it was a relief, but it usually meant that the bullies were focusing their attention on someone else. Jesse would watch other kids get picked on and see from the way they acted on the outside that they were feeling the same way as he was on the inside. Seeing others get bullied was what kept Jesse from doing what everybody else appeared to like doing: hurting one another.

One day, in grade four, Vanessa Musgrove had the misfortune of sticking an eraser up her nose. She had succeeded in concealing it from people for the better part of the day, but she grew increasingly worried. When she started to cry, everybody started laughing. She cried even more. Jesse couldn't stand to see her suffer. He felt sorry for her and made a secret pledge to never make fun of anyone. Vanessa was allowed to leave school early that day; Jesse never saw her again.

After a while, being made fun of seemed to be a part of school, as much as going to class and playing at recess. He avoided the older kids and stayed close to his friends, but he always walked home and ate lunch by himself, wishing that lunchtime was all the time.

When things got really bad, he would feign sickness.

Missing school was becoming a habit for him, but it was a habit that was necessary for his survival and today, at thirteen years of age, Jesse was feeling the need to survive.

CHAPTER THREE

Jesse heard his parents waking up across the hall. His father was usually up first; his mother soon followed. It was the same routine each and every morning, and Jesse didn't need to see them to know what they were doing.

He heard his father run the shower and, later on, open the window so that he could have a smoke. Jesse didn't like his parents smoking and had encouraged them to quit too many times over the past few years.

He couldn't understand how people could knowingly kill themselves, and he couldn't help but be reminded of all the kids that were starting to smoke at school—walking out as far as they could through the field and sharing a cigarette that someone had stolen from their older brother or sister. Afterwards, they marched into class bathed in cheap cologne, molesting a piece of gum while coughing up and swallowing their phlegm. It disgusted Jesse, and he wished his parents would stop. After weeks of nagging and throwing their cigarettes into the trash bin, he made them promised that they would quit when he graduated from elementary school. He was beginning to feel that all of their lives depended on his graduation.

After his father showered, his parents got dressed. Jesse's father went downstairs to make coffee, and his mother walked into Jesse's room to wake him up. He counted her footsteps and, just before she got to the door, let out a moan he hoped she heard, shuffled his feet, and ran his fingers over his face and through his hair. Jesse cleared his throat as if his life depended on it and quickly got into character. He had to convince his mother that he was too sick to go to school, so he imagined a fever and broke into a mild sweat. He was getting so good at pretending to be sick that sometimes he *made* himself sick and didn't have to lie.

"Good morning my little Gift! Time for school!"

Action.

"My stomach hurts, Mom." He turned to face the wall, opened his eyes, and hoped that she fell for it. Then he heard her sigh and was sorry that he worried her.

"*Again*, Jesse? This is the second time this month. You can't miss too much school, baby. You know how hard it is for you to keep up."

"Don't remind me," he groaned.

"Jesse, are you okay?"

"I'm fine, Mom. Honest. My stomach just hurts and we're not doing much at school today anyway."

The silence told Jesse that she was at least considering it.

"Okay, bud. Stay home today, but I don't want you going outside! Do you hear me?"

Jesse nodded as if he was too weak to even open his mouth and say anything.

"There's chicken soup in the cupboard, and I'll leave twenty dollars on the counter if you need anything in case of an emergency. And don't forget to feed Holly!"

Hearing her name, Holly barked and jumped up onto the bed at Jesse's feet and worked her way up his legs, swimming beneath the blankets. She came up for air on Jesse's chest and licked him on his chin.

"Are you still gonna come down for breakfast?"

"Sure."

Jesse liked to see his parents off to work each morning. Despite the fact that they left an hour and a half before he had to be up for school, he woke up each morning and lay on the couch in the living room while his parents had breakfast and a cigarette with their coffee. He liked lying there and hearing his parents talk, and he liked the smell of coffee and the sound of the spoon clinking and clanking against the inside of the mug. He liked the couch and the half-dreams that visited him as he tried to stay awake so that he could say goodbye. When they left for work, he usually fell back asleep on the sofa until his mother phoned from work to wake him up for school.

Today was Thursday, but Jesse wasn't going to school—though his mother still called to make sure that he was all right. After setting down the phone, he sat up on the couch and looked at the empty living and at the television that almost begged for power.

He liked being away from school. Jesse rubbed his hands together and licked his lips. It was time for breakfast.

He rummaged through all the cupboards and settled for a few cookies, some chips, chocolate milk, and a handful of chocolate almonds. He put a cookie back because he felt guilty, then grabbed his chocolate milk and marched over to the couch so that he could eat the way he thought every meal should be eaten—in front of the television.

"Now this is more like it!" He turned on the television, changed the channels with one hand while drinking his glass of chocolate milk from the other and belched.

"That was a good one, eh, Holly?"

If there was one thing that Jesse didn't like about being away from school, it was daytime television. It sucked. It was obvious to him that kids weren't supposed to be home during the day because of all the soap operas, games shows, talk shows, and commercials for laundry detergent and mini-vans.

But it was television and there were just too many choices for there not to be something a thirteen-year-old could watch on his day off from school.

Halfway through his chocolate almonds and another episode of Disney's *Recess*, the local news station interrupted the program.

"*We have breaking news out of . . .*"

Jesse's stomach turned. The hair on the back of his neck stood on end and he started to feel anxious.

"Not something else, man!" He reached for the remote and turned up the volume.

"*What you are looking at is the aftermath of an explosion at the American Embassy in . . .*"

Jesse sat in disbelief as the TV showed images of people broken in half, their limbs pointing in directions they shouldn't have been.

"Another damn attack!"

Over the past few months, the news had been ripe with stories about attacks in countries that Jesse didn't know much about: Iraq, Syria, Afghanistan, Yemen. There was news of car bombs, grenade attacks, rebel strikes, terrorist attacks, and suicide attacks.

It all seemed so violent and sad—someone dying, someone crying. Every station was carrying the footage of bodies being picked out of the rubble. Changing the channels couldn't change the story—A&E profiled another serial killer, and the History Channel would have a person think that the only thing that ever happened in the world was war. Nothing but violence.

Jesse was tired of watching news with the same old stories and headlines. He turned off the television, picked up his plate, and headed for the kitchen. "I think I'll go catch some fish!"

Holly growled.

"Don't worry, pooch, I won't be too long. If you don't tell on me, I'll buy you a treat!"

Holly wagged her consent.

He walked through the living room and drew the curtains so that he could see the pond that his father had built out back. Jesse asked his father for a pond after seeing one on television. He had forgotten the name of the show, but he never forgot how cool the pond had looked and did not give up until his father gave in.

Jesse liked showing it off to his cousins and friends because it was one of the few things that he had that other kids at school did not. He got into the habit of naming his fish, recognizing each one by their distinct features. In the winter he returned them to the lake; and in the spring, he set out to meet up with some old friends.

After fetching his fishing rod from the garage and fishing for his tackle under his bed, Jesse sauntered off to the lake.

He walked, careful not step on any cracks because he didn't want to break his mother's back, and counted every plane that passed by in the sky. With the twenty dollars his mother had given him, he bought some chocolate, some gum, some water, some candy, and a loaf of bread to feed the ducks with. He bought Holly a blue plastic clown that she was sure to enjoy squeezing the life out of.

At the entrance of the park, Jesse set the gear down to give his arms a rest. Standing there, he looked down the street at St. Gregory's and was happy not to be in school.

He looked at his watch.

10:53 a.m.

If he had been in school, he'd be in religion studying the New Testament and the story of Jesus. Jesse was happy to be fishing rather than reading about how much Jesus had suffered. It discouraged him at times because Jesse didn't have God for a father.

It was the third week in May, and the sky was blue and the grass was green. Jesse took a deep breath and swallowed the fresh air. He followed a path that snaked its way through the small hills that Jesse used to run down as a child. He remembered standing at the top of one hill and waiting for his father to tell him that he could take off. When he received the signal, Jesse would run down the hill, quickening his pace the closer he got to the bottom. When he hit the pavement, he imagined it was a runway and pretended to take off at full speed to join the ducks and seagulls and planes and all the angels that passed overhead.

It all seemed so long ago. *Too* long ago.

Jesse shook his head and picked up the pace.

The park was empty except for a man sitting on a bench. He was reading a book with one hand and rocking a stroller with the other. Jesse smiled and worked his way through a path outlined by trees that couldn't decide if they were alive or dead. He came out into a clearing, dropped his gear, stretched, and watched a plane fly past overhead.

"Four," Jesse counted as he watched it disappear over the rooftops of the houses that lined the pond.

He sat down on the rock and threw out his line and was happy to not be at school. He took a deep breath and tried to take it all in. It was only a few hours ago that Jesse had woken up from a dream where, in this very spot, he had tried to kill himself.

Time passed, the bucket was filled with fish, and Jesse's entire body was tuned in to the sounds of the birds and the soft breeze that ruffled the leaves on the trees. It was as if each sound was for Jesse alone—he only wished his world could sound this good all of the time.

He was giving the idea some thought when he felt a tug on the end of the line. Jesse jerked back his rod and hoped the hook was set.

When the fish was out of the water, Jesse grabbed it with his free hand and sat back on the rock so that he could take out the hook. The fish was being stubborn, and Jesse had a difficult time holding onto it.

Jesse gasped. The hook punctured the eye of the fish.

The fish didn't cry out, but it jerked its body loud enough for Jesse to hear just how much pain he had inflicted. He was about to place it in the bucket with the other fish, but didn't think a fish with one eye would be such a nice thing to look at.

He felt sorry for it, so he walked over to the pond and put it back in the water where he hoped it would heal. He watched and waited for it to swim off. It didn't.

It was dead.

Jesse looked at the dead fish and couldn't help but feel that he had somehow betrayed himself. He was reminded of school and of being made fun of because he didn't fit in, because *he* didn't look the part.

Jesse stood there mourning just long enough to see a seagull swoop down, grab the dead fish, and fly away so that it could eat in peace.

He checked on the four fish that he had caught earlier, hoping that he wasn't going to be the cause of any more pain and suffering. Happy that he had only managed to kill one thing today, he decided it was time for lunch. As if on cue, he heard the lunch bell going off at St. Gregory's.

After every last bit of food had been consumed, Jesse picked up the wrappers from the chocolate bars, shoved them into his pocket, and decided it was time to go.

He had tied up his rod and was checking around one last time to see if he had forgotten anything when he heard a branch crack and a bird cry out. The ducks that were guided by the soft spring breeze suddenly flapped their wings and headed for the trees. Jesse heard voices: two guys, maybe three. They were dragging their feet the same way they did in the halls, and Jesse knew that he was in for it. He was sorry that he didn't listen to his mother.

"Well, well, well. Look who it is," Martin Paynesworth said with feigned surprise, because he always knew he'd catch up to Jesse. Didn't see you in school today, homo! Wud you do? Play sick you so you could play with yourself all day?"

Rudy Sinclair was smoking a cigarette and laughing the same way he did every time Martin said something. The two were inseparable, and Jesse held them equally responsible for making his elementary school experience the hell that it was.

They weren't the only ones, but they were the loudest— and being loud at school counted for everything.

Jesse wasn't the only one they picked on, but it seemed that he was their favourite target. He figured that Martin was still upset because his mother didn't take a picture of him after the first day of school, and surmised that Rudy just followed Martin around because that was what he did all day.

They even looked alike: They wore baggy jeans with baggier basketball jerseys that draped over their knees. They wore their ball caps tilted to the side, a three-dollar necklace that was supposed to look like it cost a thousand, and they walked with a limp for no real reason. They called each other "gangsta" and "pimp," and even had a handshake reserved for their crew.

Jesse, Elly, and Ryan would watch them out in the playground and quietly make fun of them, running through the things that they would have said to their faces if they weren't so afraid.

Jesse needed his friends.

He knew that right now was no time for courage, so he decided to stay quiet and imagine that Martin and Rudy were no threat. It was wishful thinking.

With his fishing rod and bucket in tow, Jesse turned his back on them and began walking, but he heard their feet keep up with his and knew that he was headed for some trouble.

"Hey, wait up, loser! Here, fishy! Here, fishy-fishy!"

Jesse picked up the pace while Martin and Rudy picked up whatever they could get their hands on: empty pop cans, rocks, branches, and a beer bottle that hit Jesse in the back of his head and sent him crashing to the ground. The last thing Jesse saw was the man reading to his baby, and the last thing he felt was the side of his head hitting the concrete.

When he opened his eyes, he looked up at the empty sky and for a brief moment thought that he was an angel. Then he figured that angels wouldn't feel the pain he was now feeling. His head was throbbing, and his elbow was bleeding. He picked himself up and felt for blood on the side of his head. He wiped off his clothes and looked out at the path that led to school where he could see Martin and Rudy jumping up and down, throwing each other high-fives and flexing their biceps.

Martin turned around and put his hands around his mouth and yelled, "Have your mother take a picture of you now, you retard!"

Rudy stopped and yelled, "If you think this is bad, wait until high school!"

They continued celebrating as they turned the corner that took them back to school.

The bell rang. Jesse felt like a boxer being counted out of a fight.

Lunchtime was over.

He looked around the park. He was alone. The man that was reading to his baby was gone and the birds had flown away, afraid for their lives. Jesse wondered if the man had seen anything or if he ran when he was saw that there was going to be trouble. "So much for grown ups," Jesse lamented.

He gave his head a shake and noticed his fishing rod on the pavement, broken like the bodies he saw on the news this morning. He sighed and almost cried, but not before he saw the fish that he had just caught, crushed to death. He could see a Nike symbol stamped into the body of a fish that had been decapitated. He stared at the casualties and shook his head in disbelief, wishing he could change the channel. He wiped a tear, picked up Holly's toy, and walked home with a headache and the emptiest bucket in the world.

At home, Jesse washed himself, changed his clothes, and popped an aspirin to quell the pain. He opened the can of chicken soup that his mother had left out for him and emptied it into the toilet, wishing that he had listened to his mother. He threw Holly her toy, and turned on the television.

"We interrupt this program . . ."

Jesse watched for a few minutes, but only because he knew that changing the channel wouldn't change the story. He listened as the anchorman updated the body count and announce that a terrorist group from Afghanistan had claimed responsibility for the attacks on the Embassy. Jesse looked on as rescue workers continued to pull bodies out of the wreckage. For a brief moment, Jesse thought he saw a rescue-worker carrying a giant fish. He fell asleep until his mother came home from work and woke him up for dinner.

Jesse didn't feel like fish sticks and barely made it through his mashed potatoes.

His mother didn't see him smile all evening and grew concerned. "Baby, are you still not feeling well?"

He looked at her sitting across the table and responded with a half-hearted smile, "Mom, do I have to go to St. Elizabeth's next year?" The thought of four more years with Martin and Rudy unsettled him, and he had to figure out some way to get away from them.

"Honey, you know your father and I would prefer if you went to a Catholic school. Jesus don't work in those public schools, babe!"

"Well, St. Gregory's is a Catholic School and it looks like Jesus doesn't work there either!"

"Listen, Jesse," his mother said seriously as she set down her fork. "You're a month away from graduation. You've been through a lot since we moved out here, and we tried the best we could to get you through school. Despite all the crap that's happened, you've made it—and you made it in a Catholic school with Catholic teachers and Catholic administrators. Trust me: I've heard what goes on in those public schools."

"How could you know?" Jesse interrupted. "You haven't been to school in years. It's different now!"

"Come on, baby. You have to give it a chance!"

Breathing a sigh that signaled defeat, he took his plate from the table and headed for the kitchen.

"Hey, what happened to your elbow?" Jesse's mother asked.

"Nothing. I was playing with Holly and gave myself a rug burn. I'm going to go upstairs and study for my French test tomorrow."

He was usually careful about hiding his wounds (both emotional and physical) and secretly cursed himself for not having been more astute.

His mother got up from her seat and took her son's hands into her own. "Baby, listen to me: We went through some of the same things that you're going through now. Everybody does. You see how short your dad is . . . "

Jesse looked over at his dad, who was blushing and offering a fatherly nod.

"Well," she continued, "being short wasn't easy on him. You've a month to go, and then you're off to high school where things will be different. You'll meet new people, join teams, and maybe even run for Student Council. Then, when you graduate high school, you can start thinking about what you want to do."

"You know what I want to do!"

She walked back to her seat, picked up an envelope, looked over at Jesse and smiled. "I know what you want to do, and I have something here that's going to help you do it."

"What is it?"

She passed Jesse the envelope. "I don't know. Open it!"

She must have known, because the envelope was already open. He pulled out the letter and, when he finished reading it, looked up at his mother and father with a huge smile. His head no longer hurt, and his elbow no longer burned. Whatever had happened that day was soon forgotten as Jesse read and reread his acceptance letter to the Air Cadets.

He was one step closer to flying a plane and getting a chance to fly amongst the angels.

Chapter Four

For the first time in what seemed like ages, Jesse didn't wake with the word loser on his lips. He had a good sleep because he dreamt of flying instead of dying, and he knew that he would wake up one day closer to being a pilot. He finally had something in his life to look forward to.

Jesse lay on his back and pressed the acceptance letter over his heart like a bandage trying to stop the bleeding. He looked up at the plane hanging from a string and, for the fist time, saw it for what it really was: a toy. He was smart enough to know that toys could only take a kid so far in life.

He got up from his bed and saw his parents off to work, and then fell asleep on the couch where he slept until his mother called to tell him she loved him and that it was time for him to wake up for school.

After a quick breakfast, he sprinted up to his room two steps at a time. Before he got dressed, he turned on his CD player and pressed play.

"This is how you remind me of what I really am," Jesse sang to Nickelback as he skipped over to his closet and got ready for school.

He didn't have to think long and hard about what he was going to wear. There were plenty of jeans, khakis, dress shirts, t-shirts, golf shirts, basketball jerseys, hats, and sneakers. Jesse didn't like to put too much thought into things he wore—he had more important things to worry about. He ripped his Colorado Avalanche jersey from a hanger and picked his favourite jeans up off of the floor. He pulled his boxers over his belly button, pulled his jeans up to his hips, and looped an otherwise useless belt around the baggy pants that were now hanging from his waist for dear life.

His mother hated when he wore his pants that low, but it was in style and Jesse couldn't afford not to be. He threw his jersey over his head, scraping his knuckles on the ceiling of his room. He gave his body a shake so that the clothes fell into place and walked into the washroom for the cosmetic part of his morning routine.

He picked up his gel, squirted a blob into the palm of his hand, ran his fingers through his hair, and managed to style it without looking at his face in the mirror. He brushed his teeth and rinsed. He splashed water over his face and used the cleanser and moisturizer that his mother heard was good for acne.

He doused himself in cologne and was about to set the bottle back down when he thought another squirt might do the trick. Girls liked a boy that smelled nice. He thought about all the girls who were beginning to look like women and all the guys who couldn't stop looking at them, talking about them, or thinking about them.

And then he thought of Elly.

She was turning into a woman right before his eyes: her hair was longer, her skin soft, and her body was changing its shape. She was the most beautiful best friend in the world, and today, at lunch, Jesse was going to ask her to their graduation formal.

With a surge of confidence and the acceptance letter beside the sink, Jesse, without looking at his face, liked what he saw. He only hoped that his acne wouldn't be the focus of everyone's attention at school today.

It had come out of nowhere in grade seven. A pimple on his forehead and then on his cheek, another one on his chin and, when he woke up three days later, his face had been swarmed.

At first, no one made fun of him.

Most of the senior kids were trying to mask their own acne in some way or another, but when their faces cleared up, they started to make fun of everyone whose face hadn't. As usual, Martin and Rudy were the loudest. Jesse's academic shortcomings were no longer their focus. They didn't bother calling him retarded or stupid; instead, they found nasty things to say about his face.

Jesse felt as if his personal space was being invaded. He had tried everything—his mother spent a small fortune on scrub brushes and medicines. Some people suggested toothpaste, while his grandmother said vinegar and water would do the trick. Most were old wives tales that were too good to be true, just like zits that disappeared over the span of a commercial.

"If it works for Puff Daddy and Jessica Simpson, it can work for you, too."

But the expensive medicines didn't work, and the magic potions were never magical enough.

Jesse was losing hope and starting to think that he'd have to deal with acne his whole life—and he was growing increasingly desperate because of it.

It was Elly that suggested the most outlandish of all remedies.

"You should try foundation, Jesse!" She could see by the look in his eyes that putting on make-up was simply not an option for a teenage boy who was having a difficult enough time growing up. "If it works for girls, it can work for you, too," she persisted.

Later that evening, Jesse rifled through his mother's make up bag and stood, half an hour later, in front of a mirror with a brown face and white neck.

"This is ridiculous, man!" Jesse drowned his face in water and watched the foundation seep into the sink. He had thought about how he looked with acne so much over the past couple of years that he was beginning to forget how he had looked without it.

He did come up with the idea of having his school photos touched up so that he could see himself, see his face, clear and clean. He looked at those touched-up photos more often than he looked in the mirror. He knew he was kidding himself, but it felt good to look like everyone else—if only in a picture that hung from the wall.

But Jesse no longer wanted to think about his acne. Instead, he looked down at his acceptance letter. "I can't believe I got in! I'm gonna be a pilot!"

Jesse downed his Ritalin with a palmful of lukewarm water. He wiped his mouth, put on his shoes, found his keys (but forgot his books), locked the door, and tried to figure out how he was going to ask Elly to the grad.

He marched to school and forgot about yesterday and the dead fish. Instead, he thought about today and, with no trepidation, walked past the park where the innocent fish were slaughtered. He felt like it happened so long ago, because he had spent all of last night looking into the future and imagining finally getting a chance to fly. He carried the acceptance letter in his back pocket like soldiers did medals on their chests.

Like they had promised, Ryan and Elly were waiting for him out front. Ryan was looking at his watch, and Elly must have been looking for Jesse because when she saw him, she smiled and ran up to him and jumped into his arms. She kissed Jesse on the forehead and kept her hands perched upon his shoulders.

"I heard about what happened yesterday. Are you okay?"

"I guess word travels quickly."

"You know it does!"

Jesse looked at Ryan and could tell that something was wrong. "What's the matter with him?"

"He fell asleep last night studying for French and—"

"And if I don't pass, my dad won't let me go to Cadets! I got my letter yesterday, and now I might not be able to go! Did you get yours?"

"In my back pocket, baby!" Jesse tapped his back pocket to make sure it was still there.

The sound of the bell unnerved Jesse. He thought about yesterday and Martin and Rudy, and he hoped that today would be better than yesterday. He took one last look at the sky. His eyes fell on the crucifix, looking as if it were holding up the entire sky, the same way it did from his bedroom window yesterday morning. His stomach turned, but he thought about cadets and headed for first period class.

Parents didn't send their kids to St. Gregory's because it had a particularly good reputation or because a decision had been made after hours and hours of research.

If a family lived north of the highway and east of the river, they went here; if they lived west of the beer store and south of the Tim Horton's, they went there.

The mortgage was paid, the driveway paved, and the fence was being built next week. Here or there, the only choice to be made was whether or not they wanted to send their kids to a Catholic school or a public one.

For Jesse's parents, there was nothing to think about.

"Jesus doesn't work in them other schools!" he heard his mother proclaim far too many times after Jesse had asked her if he could switch schools.

Inside, there were bathrooms, classrooms, a staff room, and a broom closet. The gym had two basketball nets and ropes that the kids in grade three were terrified of climbing. It was a small school with plenty of students and not enough portables.

The most popular spot in the school was the cafeteria, and Jesse tried to avoid it all costs. Where you sat was determined by a number of factors: the colour of your skin, the style of music you listened to, the clothes you wore, the grade you were in, and the people you knew. Territories were clearly marked, reminding Jesse of a show that he had seen on the Discovery Channel where animals marked their territory and put up a fight when anyone crossed its bounds.

The cafeteria served more than food—it served bullying with a side order of gravy. It was the one place in the whole school where students convened daily. It was a chance to be seen. Before students ate their lunch, some girls would run to the washroom to check their hair, while some boys ran to their lockers for another shot of cologne. Boys strutted like pigeons in front of the girls, and the girls hoped they blushed enough to get the pigeons to look at them.

There were plenty of fights, finger pointing, and throwing pieces of food to get a person's attention. The only time they all seemed to communicate with one another was when everyone took pleasure in someone being picked on. Like the day Brenda Saunders, a heavy-set girl with very few friends, fell through the bench she was sitting on. The entire school laughed, a few even applauded. Jesse tried to help, but he was held back by the crowd that encircled her.

Rumours of extortion were rampant inside the school, but nobody could prove a thing because no one would come forward with a perpetrator's name. Jesse avoided the cafeteria as much as he could.

The only place Jesse feared more than the cafeteria was the hall.

He could avoid the cafeteria, but he couldn't avoid the halls. He had to hang up his coat, go to the bathroom, head off to class, go out for recess, and go home at the end of the day.

In the mornings the hallways were congested with students walking and talking to the person beside them or on their cell phones. They stopped to talk to friends, trying to find out who was selling what and who had just broken up with whom. Teachers ushered the masses to the classes as music played through the overhead speakers. Many were late for class, walking in during Morning Prayer to the death stare of their homeroom teacher.

There were sixty-three teachers, three administrators and twelve support workers on the staff at St. Gregory's. The ten years that Jesse had been in elementary school were tough on everyone involved in the education system, not just the students.

The government wanted to hold schools more accountable, so they increased academic expectations and based school funding on student achievement and overall school performance.

Money was tight, and students had to make due with less.

Last year, St. Gregory's implemented a policy where a student could only be given a new pencil if the old one was less than an inch long. Some of the older kids took to dealing pencils in the hallways at a huge mark-up.

There were walkouts, work-to-rules, and the threat of a lockout. There was a lot of yelling and screaming, and sometimes the teachers would use words they encouraged their students to avoid. The teachers said the government was bullying them, and the government said that they weren't. To Jesse, they all sounded more like kids than adults.

Missing a day and then coming back was never easy.

Not only did Jesse have to get caught up on the work he missed yesterday, but he also had to complete the activities for the day and finish his homework for tomorrow. Despite the heavy workload, it had been a good day for Jesse.

Martin and Rudy were both away, and the other members of their clique were too busy playing dice and quarters to take notice of him. When Martin and Rudy were away, there was always less tension in the halls and out in the yard. With no threat of violence, everybody went back to being a kid.

But there were always those few silhouettes that stood out in the distance, waiting for something—anything—to happen.

At recess, Jesse played soccer. He scored three goals and was particularly happy because Elly was watching and cheering him on. After each one of his goals, she jumped up and down, her pigtails flailing at the mercy of her excitement. She pumped her fist into the air and, with the other hand, cupped her mouth and shouted, "Way to go, Jesse!"

He looked over at her and, even though she was over half a soccer field away, he knew she was still the most beautiful best friend in the world, and he was her biggest fan.

He was starting to like Elly in a more-than-a-friend kind of way, and he didn't know what to do about it. Ryan told him to tell her, but Jesse was too shy. Besides, he had seen the disastrous results of friends dating in the movies and on television.

He and Elly were really close, and they liked to watch *Friends* together on Thursday evenings. Jesse's favourite episode was the one with the graduation video, where Monica was still fat and Ross fell in love with Rachel.

Jesse stood out on the pitch watching Elly jump up and down and he couldn't help but be reminded of the day he fell in love with her.

It was a warm Saturday afternoon. Jesse was outside counting the planes that passed overhead when he saw the moving truck come down the street and back up into a driveway seven houses down from his own. After he finished his lunch, Jesse went back outside, hoping to catch a glimpse of his new neighbours. He looked down the street and saw a girl sitting on a couch waiting to be picked up and brought into the house.

Her hair was pulled back into pigtails with pink bows, and her hands were in her lap. She was kicking her feet in anticipation, hoping that someone would pick up the couch and carry her into her castle like a princess.

Jesse's mother sent him over with some popsicles, which eventually melted all over the couch because they were too busy laughing. Elly's mother pretended not to notice.

They spent that whole summer together—back when girls could hang out with boys and no one would think a thing about it. When Ryan came back from the cottage that year, the three of them played in the park and swam too soon after eating things they shouldn't have.

After recess, Ryan failed his French test because he could only answer three out of the fifteen questions. Jesse was sure that he passed, and Elly didn't really care if she did or didn't. She hated French and so did her parents, so she really didn't have anything to worry about. After sitting through another science lab, it was lunchtime, and today they agreed to go to Jesse's place. They were going to figure out their plans for graduation, and Jesse was going to ask Elly to be his date.

Over lunch, Jesse felt nauseous. He was sweating profusely, but hoped and prayed that Elly didn't notice. He couldn't eat any of the chips or chocolate almonds that he had set out on the table.

After careful consideration they decided to hire a limo, and they also agreed to ask their parents for an extension on their curfew. They thought one in the morning was reasonable.

All that was left to discuss was who they were taking.

Ryan wasn't so sure. He thought about asking Melanie Camara, but he heard her parents wouldn't let her date anyone that wasn't Portuguese. Takisha Wilson wasn't Portuguese, but she was black, and Ryan's father would flip his lid if he found out that his son thought a black girl was hot.

Ryan couldn't decide, but he looked over at Jesse and winked. He pointed with his chin at Elly, tilting his head in her direction. Elly was too busy flipping through a magazine to pay attention to the mime presentation.

"Cameron Diaz is *so* damn beautiful!"

She looked at Jesse and then over at Ryan.

"What?" she asked, setting the magazine aside. "What's wrong?"

The silence was beginning to annoy her. "I swear to God, if you don't tell me what's the matter I'll—"

"Tell her, Jesse!"

Jesse looked at her, and she looked at him. She was curious, and he was nervous. He was angry that Ryan had put him on the spot like this. He would have asked her when he was ready—he thought he had been.

"I . . . I—"

Jesse watched Elly reach into her purse and pull out her cell phone.

"Hello? Hey! Hold on guys," she said as she walked into the living room and around the corner, out of their sight.

"I thought those things were supposed to promote communication!" Jesse complained. He looked over at Ryan and punched him from across the table. "You idiot!"

Ryan grimaced and rubbed his shoulder. "I was only trying to help you, loser!"

"Well, don't. I hate it when you do stuff like that."

Elly came back to the kitchen and put her phone back in her purse. "Guess what, guys?"

They looked at her and then at each other.

"Chris Evanston just asked me to the grad."

Jesse didn't need to see his face to know that he had gone pale.

"What's the matter, Jesse? Don't you like him?"

He liked him all right—Chris was the coolest guy to ever go to St. Gregory's. He was tall and smart and had great hair and was good in science and english and was the best athlete to ever attend their school. Chris was also a year older than them, so every guy younger than him had been happy to see him graduate—including Jesse.

"What did you say?" Ryan asked.

The three seconds that it took for her to respond were the longest three seconds in Jesse's life.

"I said yes. What do you think I said?" She picked up the magazine and looked at Cameron Diaz. "Now I definitely have to get this dress."

Jesse couldn't focus in class the rest of the day. For the past two weeks in English, Jesse had been reading *Anne Frank: the Diary of a Young Girl*. He empathized with Anne and how she had lived her life in fear. He couldn't understand why so many people had been persecuted or how the rest of the world simply sat back and did nothing.

After reading a few sections out loud, Mr. Haines walked to the front of the room and asked the class to put down their books and pay attention. The tone of his voice was serious. "Class, today we're going to talk about yesterday's tragic events. First off, does anyone know what a terrorist attack is?" He looked around. No one raised their hand.

Jesse recalled the images he had seen on the news: the bodies, the mothers crying for their children, and the husbands promising revenge. He remembered the dead fish scattered across the path and Martin and Rudy celebrating out in the distance.

Mr. Haines shook his head. "It doesn't surprise me. These days, if something doesn't happen in your backyard, you have no idea that it happened. There were a lot of gruesome images shown on television last night and this morning, and we thought that some of you might have some questions."

It was obvious that some of the kids had no idea what he was talking about. Tanya thought he was talking about *The Bachelorette*, and Tony thought it might have had something to do with last night's episode of *Fear Factor*.

Mr. Haines talked about the number of dead and the possible reasons why such a tragedy had taken place. He mentioned the possibility of war and how, because of it, they were going to have a bomb drill.

He took them through the motions of crawling beneath the desk and showed them how curl up into a ball. Jesse had been assigned the duty of opening all the windows, which would prevent glass from flying everywhere. Mr. Haines concluded that the terrorists' main objective was to disrupt the lives of those they considered to be the enemy.

Jesse thought about Rudy and Martin and wondered how they would have reacted to the news that they were held in the same regard as terrorists. He thought about the dead fish and wondered how many casualties there needed to be before people started talking about bullying on a local level, instead of just an historical or global one.

After school, Jesse worked on his homework. He was in his room and on the computer when his mom got home from work.

She walked upstairs and was happy to see her son.

"Baby, Daddy can't take you to get your suit tonight. I have to. So we'll have a quick bite to eat and we'll go right after supper. Okay?"

"Sure, Mom."

"Come downstairs and have snack."

"In a second, Mom, I'm just on the computer." Jesse listened to her walk down the stairs, then he turned to face his computer screen.

It was 4:00 p.m. and MSN was just as congested as the halls at school. Chat was ripe with Friday-night plans and talk of graduation. It was still a month away, but the hype was off to a quick start—like trailers in December for a movie set to open in July.

Graduation was the Oscar Night of elementary school, but instead of watching people all dolled up and walking down the red carpet, the students would be the ones doing the walking, posing, dancing, laughing, and celebrating.

They chatted about the best place to get tans, corsages, tuxedos, dresses, make-up, liquor, and the cheapest hotel rooms. Jesse was about to turn off his computer when out of the corner of his eye he saw his name. *BigPimp* was telling everyone about a new acne product Jesse Cullen should try and encouraging others with acne to do the same or they'd "be sure to suffer the same fate as puke-face. LOL!"

It was Martin or Rudy. Jesse could hear the tone of their voice through the words they wrote. He turned off his computer to join his mother for supper and couldn't stop thinking about his suit for graduation. If so much of elementary school wasn't right, he wanted to make sure his big send off would be.

CHAPTER FIVE

The Convention Centre was crowded and hot. After sitting through too many speeches, more awards, and three songs by the school choir, it was finally time for the graduates to accept their diplomas.

Jesse's mother gasped when she heard her son's name. She watched him walk up the stairs and across the stage and was reminded of his first day of school and how she watched him run from the back of the bus to the front. A tear swelled in her eye as Jesse accepted his diploma. She jumped from her seat and gave her son a standing ovation, almost forgetting to take a picture.

It was a perfect evening. Not even the sight of Martin and Rudy accepting their diplomas could unsettle Jesse. He was happy that his mother was happy, and he was happy that school was over—even if only for a couple of months.

On the way out of the Convention Centre, Principal Edwards stopped Jesse and his parents. He smiled and offered his congratulations.

"It was a tough ten years son, but you made it." He reached out to shake Jesse's hand. Jesse wasn't going to take it, but his mother pinched his arm.

"Thank you, Sir," he mumbled, but he didn't mean it. In Jesse's mind there was nothing to thank him for.

Mr. Edwards was in charge of St. Gregory's. Jesse held him partially responsible for the things that happened to him. He lost count of the number of times he and his mother had sat in the office and listened to Principal Edwards make up excuse after excuse for the things that were happening in his school:

In grade two it was: "They're just being kids."

In grade four: "It'll play itself out."

Grade five: "It's just a phase."

Grade six: "It'll play itself out."

Grade seven: "I've spoken with their parents."

Two months ago: "They'll grow out of it!"

Jesse was sorry that he had shaken his hand. He turned his back on Principal Edwards as if he was turning his back on his childhood, then he left the Convention Centre holding onto his diploma for dear life.

The Cullen house was overflowing with people: His mother's brother and his father's sister were there with their families and cameras, as was Ryan's father and his new girlfriend, and what appeared to be Elly's entire extended family. The house was buzzing with anticipation as they waited for the limo that would come and pick up the kids that were one step closer to being all grown up.

Jesse, Elly, and Ryan were dateless. Chris Evanston had decided he was way too cool to go to a grade eight graduation and cancelled on Elly three nights earlier. Ryan couldn't think of anyone his father would approve of, so he settled for going stag. Meanwhile, Jesse couldn't imagine going to the grad with anyone but Elly, so he decided to let fate take its course when Chris bailed on her. She didn't know it, but tonight she was Jesse's date, and he was honoured to be going with someone so beautiful. When he saw her walk across the stage at the grad ceremony earlier that evening, she was the most beautiful girl he had ever seen.

Jesse would have rather missed the ceremony all together, but his mother told him that there was no way she wasn't going to see her son get his diploma.

"I never finished high school, baby. To know that you're on your way makes me feel a little bit better about that fact."

It was the least Jesse could do for her; she looked forward to these moments almost more than he did. She was tired of seeing him cry and making up excuses so that he wouldn't have to go to school. She understood that growing up was a lot more work than it should have been for a thirteen-year-old boy, but here he was tonight: one step closer to being the man she knew he could be.

Jesse felt good about giving his mother an opportunity to be proud of him.

The three graduates were restless and thankful to be on their way; their parents were reluctant to let them go, wishing their children would stick around and be children for a few moments longer.

When Jesse turned to say goodbye to his mother, she started to cry. Jesse hugged her and held her in his arms. He turned his head and she could feel his breath as he told her he loved her. "I couldn't have done it without you, Ma!"

Mary kissed his face in as many places as she could, squeezed his cheeks, and took a picture like she had on his first day of school. "My Gift made it!"

He shook hands with his father and headed for the door. His mother threw out her hand for one last caress and wished her son a good night, then watched him walk out the house a graduate of grade eight.

Jesse was elated. It wasn't because he had passed into high school; he was feeling good because he had survived elementary school. This milestone reminded Jesse of another promise his mother had made.

Before getting into the limo, he turned around to look at his parents. "Remember your promise!"

His parents smiled as they watched the limo drive away. They shut the door and went into the backyard to smoke their last few cigarettes.

Once in the limo and finally on their way to the party, the boys took off their jackets, and Elly kicked off her shoes. "I didn't think looking good would hurt so badly." She massaged her foot and looked up to Cameron Diaz even more.

Jesse couldn't take his eyes off her. Her hair was pulled back and her earrings tickled her bare shoulders. Her pale skin had a glow from the shiny green of her dress and her smile made him gush. Jesse recalled the photo of Cameron Diaz in a similar dress and didn't think there was much of a comparison, and told her so.

Elly blushed. "You don't look so bad yourself!"

It was the first suit Jesse had ever worn. He felt like a movie star and wanted to wear it often.

"Guys, I don't mean to interrupt, but my asshole father said I looked good, too, you know." Jesse and Elly apologized and looked Ryan up and down.

"You do look good, man!" Elly admitted.

"Hey, are you going to be allowed to go to Cadets?" asked Jesse, reaching into the inside of his coat pocket. He pulled out his acceptance letter and checked to make sure that he was still going.

"I don't think so. My father thinks it would do me some good to stay home and go to work with him for a few days a week to make money and appreciate hard work and shit—all because I failed a lousy French test!"

Ryan never looked a person in the eye when he spoke about his father. This saddened Jesse; he felt sorry for his best friend.

Jesse looked over at Ryan and thought about all the good times growing up. He remembered them as six-year-olds, when they flew kites and tried to throw tennis balls as high up into the sky as they could. The best days were the ones where they were convinced that the ball had reached the clouds. They had vivid imaginations and indulged in being children, until Ryan's father decided that it was time for him to be a man.

Ryan's dad was tough because his wife had left him with two little boys. Ryan didn't know where his mother was, but wished his father would get lost. They had the most terrible arguments, and there were times when Jesse had to leave Ryan's house because he was afraid that things were going to get violent.

Jesse had always hoped that things would get better, but they only looked to be getting worse. Things may have not been changing at home, but it was starting to look to Jesse that Ryan was.

Last year, he stole two of his father's beers and brought them over to Jesse's house. Jesse refused his and watched Ryan down them both in a matter of minutes.

Ryan was also acting up in school and was suspended for three days for telling off the head custodian, Mr. Inzahgi.

They were silent in the limo for a couple of seconds, when Ryan suddenly perked up and reached into his pocket. "I can't believe I almost forgot!"

He held up a joint as if it were some sort of relic that the whole world should admire. "If I can't get high this summer, at least I can get high tonight, baby!"

Elly and Jesse sat there hypnotized by the twisted white paper stuffed with weed. They had never smoked pot before and already felt as if they were breaking the law.

"Hey, you can't smoke that in here!" Jesse protested. He looked over at Elly and then up front at the limo driver— his heart was racing. He had seen kids smoking it at school and was even offered a dime bag by some students from St. Elizabeth's. They looked nothing like the drug dealers that

Jesse had seen on television and in movies. They were in full uniform; some of them even wore ties.

They yelled things like: "My school is a high school, and if you're coming to my school, you *gotta* get high, baby!" It was becoming the 'in' thing to do.

Elly grabbed the joint and held it to her nose. "It smells funny!"

Jesse took it and did the same. It smelled like Rudy and Martin and their entire crew after they returned from one of their trips out past the soccer field. To Jesse, they smelled like skunk.

At first he had thought they were smoking cigarettes, but they held the smoke in longer and passed the thing around a lot quicker, as if it was a treat that was to be equally shared. They came back smelling funny and acting even funnier. They laughed at everything and went straight to the cafeteria to get some food. It was only after watching an episode of *That 70's Show* that Jesse realized it must have been pot they were smoking.

He threw the joint into Ryan's lap.

Ryan put it back into his pocket. "Don't worry, dude! It's for later."

"Where'd ya get it?" Elly asked.

He had stumbled across his brother's stash while looking for a pen. Ryan took a pinch and prayed that Adam wouldn't notice. His brother was as tough on him as his dad was, and Ryan looked at this as a good way to get back at him for all the name-calling and punches.

The thought of getting high frightened Jesse. It was like he was looking at a naked woman for the first time, and he turned his head because he felt ashamed. He thought about what his mother would think if her little Gift came home stoned.

The limo pulled up to the entrance of the hall, and everyone that was outside stopped what they were doing to stare at the limo. Ryan could see the looks on their faces and was glad that he had made an impression.

'Now that's what I call an entrance, baby!"

Elly pulled out her mirror from her purse and applied one more layer of lipstick. Jesse ran his fingers through his hair and straightened the creases on his jacket.

"This is it, guys. We made it, and tonight we're going to celebrate!"

The hall was dark, the music was loud, and strobe lights lit the way to the dance floor. Jesse and Elly found a table, and Ryan went to get some drinks.

When Ryan returned, Elly left to dance with some of her girlfriends.

Ryan gave Jesse his drink and sat down. He nudged Jesse with his elbow. "Are you gonna say anything to her tonight?"

Jesse didn't answer. Things were good as they were, and he knew it was only a matter of time before he and Elly hooked up.

Everyone was at the top of their game, feeling like a million bucks on a budget of two hundred. Graduates were dancing and laughing, moving around the dance floor and congratulating one another. Girls stopped every couple of feet and smiled on three so that someone else could take a picture, then went on their way hoping someone else would ask for another picture and a dance.

Jesse and Ryan stared out at the crowd, pointing at all the girls and laughing at few of the boys. Most people were dancing, and more than a few of them shouldn't have been. Tony Di Marco looked like a statue trying to move its feet; Cassandra Jordan broke a heel and rolled her ankle, but still got up and gave it a shot.

Ryan laughed. "You've gotta admire her resilience, eh?"

Jesse had never seen so many of his classmates laughing all at once. They may have sat in different parts of the cafeteria and kept to certain parts of the playgrounds, but tonight they were all graduates and, for once, felt like they belonged to something bigger than themselves.

Jesse felt the same way, but only wished they had realized it a lot sooner. He set down his pop and went to ask Elly for dance.

The DJ announced that it was lights on in half an hour. The dance floor voiced its displeasure and danced like their time together was almost up.

Elly, shoeless and getting lost in the song, asked Jesse if he could get her a drink. As Jesse turned his back on her, he felt Elly's hand on his shoulder. When he turned around, she stood on her tiptoes and planted a kiss on his cheek.

Jesse blushed. "What was that for?"

"For being you, that's all!" She continued dancing and Jesse fell deeper in love with her. He could still feel her lips on his cheek as he walked up to the bar and ordered two drinks.

Jesse leaned on the bar and bounced his head to a song he had a heard a million times on the radio but couldn't figure out the title. It was on the tip of his tongue when he looked out on the dance floor and saw Ryan showing Bobby Williams and Reggie Caulfield the joint.

Jesse had a feeling that Ryan was just as happy to be graduating as he was.

At school, kids made fun of Ryan because he was clumsy, because he didn't have a mother, and because he hung out with a 'faggot' and a 'dike'. Jesse always worried that Ryan was going to snap. He had talked about bringing a bat to school, and one day told Jesse that he was going to bring a knife and kill someone. It took Ryan a full two minutes to finally come around and admit that he was just joking.

Jesse was still navigating the dance floor when he spotted Martin and Rudy. He stood there, not noticing his drinks on the bar, when he saw Rudy empty a bottle into his plastic cup while Martin kept an eye on the chaperones.

Jesse shook his head. "Those guys may be graduating, but they didn't learn a damn thing!" He hoped they would over the course of the summer. If it wasn't for those two, he might have actually looked forward to high school.

Teachers may have run the classrooms, but those two ran the halls and playgrounds. They played God and made everyone's life hell, acting like gangsters from all the movies they loved to quote and lyrics they liked to rap. They entertained and scared people into liking them. *Scarface* was their favourite movie, Snoop Dog and Jay-Z, their favourite rappers. The playground was their block; the hallways, their streets.

Jesse was getting flustered, but remembered where he was, why he was there, and what he was going to be doing in a couple of weeks.

He took the drinks from the bar and went and sat with Ryan and Elly.

At 11:45 p.m. the lights were turned on, and the congregation let out a collective sigh. Everyone was sweating, not looking nearly as good as when they first arrived. The smoke machine was stinging their eyes as they tried to find their purses and jackets and say goodbye for the summer.

On their way out, Ryan suddenly stopped and pointed. "Hey, look at tough guy over there!"

Jesse turned to see Martin throwing up into a potted plant. Elly took each of the boys' arms and led them out the doors—graduates of grade eight.

The limousine cruised down the streets with Ryan, Elly, and Jesse sprawled out in the back. Elly's head was on Jesse's chest, who was stretched out on the couch, looking through the open sun roof and trying to make sense of the stars that streaked by.

"Well, guys, we made it," Jesse said with a sigh of relief.

"Fucking right we did, man! Off to high school, baby!" Ryan exclaimed.

Elly turned her head and asked, "What are you so excited about high school for? You're at the bottom of the food chain again."

"Elly, I don't wanna think about that shit right now. I'm excited . . . because of chicks! Lots and lots of chicks!" Ryan screamed at the top of his lungs.

"Yeah—too bad your dad won't let you date any of them!"

Elly and Jesse laughed.

"Screw my dad, man!" Ryan reached into his pocket with his father on his mind and tempted Jesse and Elly to help him settle the score.

"Let's smoke this!" Ryan banged on the window and asked the driver to pull over.

It was the first time any of them had ever smoked a joint.

Jesse didn't know what to do with himself. He couldn't decide if he liked what he was feeling. It felt like a balloon had replaced his brain and he had trouble holding on to a thought.

Elly sat at the end of the park bench and listened to Ryan babble as he hung from the monkey bars. She giggled and was happy that she decided to smoke pot for the first time.

Jesse, suddenly craving a handful of chocolate-covered almonds, was worried about his curfew. "Does anyone know what time it is?" he asked, hoping he didn't have to be home anytime soon.

Ryan loosened his grip and planted his feet on the ground, losing his balance for a second. "Its who-the-hell-cares-what-time-it-is time!" Ryan laughed and looked at the two of them. His face was now stern, and he looked as if he had something profound to say.

"Guys, I want high school to be different for us next year."

Elly looked at him. "What do you mean, stoner?"

"I don't know. Just . . . different."

Jesse knew what he was talking about, but was too worried about breaking his curfew to get into it. "Hey, I want high school to be different, too, but I won't make it to high school if I break my curfew. What times it?" Jesse asked, getting more and more paranoid with each falling star.

Ryan grew annoyed. "You know something, Jesse? You should really try and grow up a little. You know, live a little, man!"

When they reached Ryan's house just before 1 a.m., Ryan reached into his pocket and pulled out a bottle of Visine. "Put this in your eyes. I stole it from my brother, too."

Jesse missed a few times before he got it right and passed it over to Elly. The three of them stood there with fake tears falling down their cheeks and couldn't help but laugh at how silly they must have looked.

They had a group hug and promised to meet tomorrow for lunch.

It was a beautiful night, and the stars were the only witness to Jesse and Elly's late-night jaunt. They walked down the empty streets like it was a carpet laid just for them. Elly was barefoot. Jesse carried her shoes. She rested her head on Jesse's shoulder.

"Are you still stoned?" she asked.

"Not really."

She let out a sigh and was silent for a moment. "So what did ya think?"

"About the grad?"

Elly giggled. "No! About the weed, dummy!"

"It wasn't anything special. I liked it, but I wouldn't want to be stoned at school. I don't know how those guys did it!"

"Who? Martin and Rudy?" Elly asked. "They didn't, man! They almost failed." Jesse wished that they had.

"I hear there's a lot weed going around in high school."

"I hear a lot of things are going around in high school." Jesse changed the subject. The last thing he wanted to think about was Martin and Rudy. "Ryan's funny, eh?"

"Yeah, a real madman. Just like his father!"

Jesse turned to walk her to the door, but Elly grabbed his hand and sat down on the curb, pulling him down beside her. She rested her head on his shoulder and tightened her grip around his hand.

Jesse looked down at their interlocked hands.

She was caressing her thumb against his when Jesse caught a glimpse of movement on her cheek. A tear worked its way down her face and fell off her chin, landing on the back of his hand.

"Hey, what's wrong with you?" Jesse pulled her closer and ran his fingers up and down the nape of her neck.

"I'm just so happy to be out of that place, Jesse!"

"Me, too, baby. Me, too!" Jesse held her tighter and tried to reassure her: "If it's no better in high school, at least we'll still have each other, Elly!"

She lifted her head off of his shoulder and looked him in the eyes. Jesse smiled, but he could see that there was something else. Jesse was still a little stoned and paranoid.

"Jesse, I have something to tell you, but I don't think you're going to like it."

He looked at her and smirked. "What?"

"You know how I told you that Miss Costa was impressed with my art?"

"Yeah, she said you had some serious talent."

"Well, she got me a scholarship for The Academy of Arts and—," Elly stopped and took a deep breath. "I won't be going to St. Elizabeth's next year. I didn't want to tell you tonight, but I can't stop thinking about it. The pot really screwed me up there for a sec."

Jesse was silent. He didn't know what to say.

She had mentioned the possibility of going to another school a few months back, but he buried the memory of that day the same way he tried to bury the memories of all his bad days. A lump formed in Jesse's throat and he did what he could to hold back a tear.

"Why are you so upset? That's great news, Elly."

She wiped her nose with the base of her wrist and put her head back on his shoulder. "I was just hoping that we'd get to go to high school together. That's all. I don't know what I would have done if you weren't at St. Gregory's."

Jesse felt the same way and told her. He was happy for her, but he was sad for himself. He did the right thing and congratulated her. "Besides, there's always next season."

Elly was confused. "Next season? Whada'ya mean?"

"Nothing," Jesse responded as he looked at his Rachel. He reminded her what time it was. "We better be getting home."

Jesse stood up and put out his hand for Elly.

"I had a really good time tonight, Jesse." Elly took his hand, stood up, and straightened out her dress.

"Me, too." Jesse watched her walk inside her house, and when her door closed, Jesse's heart jumped. He whispered another goodbye and headed home.

Jesse no longer felt like being all dressed up. He was happy to be getting out of the suit—he wanted the night to end. Elly was going to a different school, and he was finished with grade eight. He wanted to put an end to one life and wake up one day closer to the beginning of a new one. He walked into the washroom, took a quick look in the mirror, and pointed and winked at himself. "You look good!"

The words sounded so foreign coming out of his mouth.

He felt good about looking good and walked into his parent's bedroom to tell them about his night. His father was snoring, but his mother was in bed reading. When she saw her little gift, she put the book down and smiled. "How was your night, baby?"

Jesse walked over to the bed and told his mother about the dance. After he kissed her good night, he got up to go back to his room, but then remembered their deal. "Remember, Mom. No cigarettes tomorrow!"

"I know, baby. I know."

Once in his room, he took off his suit and put it back on the hanger as delicately as he had when he took it off. Standing in nothing but his boxers and t-shirt, Jesse looked at the suit and looked forward to having another opportunity to wear it.

He walked back into the washroom, ran the water, and leaned into the mirror to get a closer look at his face. His eyes were red and he had forgotten that he was stoned. He hoped that he hadn't remembered it out loud and that his mother hadn't smelled it on him.

Shutting off the bathroom light, Jesse went to bed a little sad, a little stoned, but still happy that elementary school was over. It was time to sleep off the past ten years and wake up one day closer to his dream of flying a plane.

He closed his eyes and imagined Elly's lips and kissed them. He missed her already. "Closest thing to an angel," he whispered. For the first time since he first uttered the phrase, Jesse wasn't talking about planes.

CHAPTER SIX

It was the first day of summer holidays, and it was hot. With elementary school behind them and high school too far away to pose any real threat, Jesse, Ryan, and Elly began their holidays the same way they did every other summer holiday: hanging out at the park and trying to avoid any thoughts of school.

But it wasn't long before high school occupied their thoughts and conversation.

Jesse sat quietly as Elly and Ryan argued.

Ryan was going on about the school uniform and how it wasn't right that they were obliged to wear one.

"Well, you could go to a public school, Ryan."

Ryan looked at Elly and laughed. "My father says that Jesus is my only hope. I don't have a choice!"

"At least everyone will look the same!" Jesse proclaimed.

Ryan looked at him and snickered. "If you think wearing a uniform is going to change things, Jesse, you're in for a huge shock!"

Elly didn't like the tone of Ryan's voice. "What makes you an expert on high school, Ryan?"

Jesse was trying to imagine himself in a uniform and what high school without Elly was going to be like.

"My brother says high school is the toughest place he's ever been, and that he was actually looking forward to going to work with our dad. One day, I walked into his room to borrow a CD. Adam was in bed, wearing his uniform and crying. I almost felt sorry for the guy—until he threatened to kill me if I told anyone. He may hate my dad, but he hated high school even more!"

Elly rolled her eyes. "Okay, okay. Let's lighten up for a second, man! It's the first day of summer, not the first day of school!"

They gathered their things and walked over to the baseball diamond and sat in a circle around home base.

"Do you guys realize," Jesse started, "that this is going to be our first summer apart from one another?"

Ryan would be working, Elly would be heading up to her new cottage, and Jesse would be on his way to flying a plane.

Jesse's stomach turned. He had a feeling that they weren't just saying goodbye to one another. In a small way, he felt as if they were saying goodbye to something much bigger. He felt as if their childhood was almost coming to an end.

When it was time to part, Jesse hugged Ryan and didn't want to let go.

"Don't spend all of your money in one place, man," Jesse warned him.

"Don't worry. I won't," Ryan responded, even though he planned to do just that.

Jesse and Elly walked home; Jesse walked particularly slowly because it was going to be a long time before he got the chance to see her again.

Once at her house, the two of them faced each other and stood silent for a few seconds.

"Listen, Jesse, before I forget . . . " Elly reached into her purse and pulled out a pair of aviator sunglasses, the kind that Jesse wanted after seeing Tom Cruise in *Top Gun*.

"These are for me? Thanks Elly!" He took them from her and put them on. "How do I look?"

"Well, seeing that I got them at the Goodwill, not that bad. Not bad at all!" She leaned into him and gave him a kiss on the cheek. "You have a good summer, Jesse. And be careful with all that flying."

Jesse thanked her. He saluted her and wished he could tell her that he loved her and already missed her. He watched her walk inside, wanting to look at her for as long as he could.

"Closest thing to an angel, man!" Jesse picked up his bike and pretended that his street was a runway, his bike a plane, and that he was Maverick getting ready for take off.

There were a few things Jesse needed to do before he left, so he woke up early the next day and got to it. He rifled through his closet to make sure he didn't forget his Avalanche jersey, his favourite jeans and sneakers, and his lucky t-shirt. He zipped up his gym bag and threw it in the pile with his others. Looking at the luggage, he suddenly realized that he had been so caught up in flying a plane that he forgot just how long he was going to be away from his parents.

He had slept at Ryan's house a few nights, but they were only one-night affairs.

This time he was going to be gone for six weeks.

He was so nervous that he felt like telling his mother he no longer wanted to go. But as he looked at his pictures from school, he realized he couldn't let all his hard work go to waste. Jesse thanked his mother for convincing him to go school that first day. He just wished he had had an easier time of things. His goal wasn't to simply pass classes and graduate, or to meet new friends, or to learn new things; his goal was to survive so that one day he could fly a plane.

The ironic thing was that he had Martin and Rudy to thank for introducing him to the Cadets. One day during recess, Martin and Rudy were making fun of Jesse, telling him that his acne was bad because he masturbated too much. Ryan was away that day and Elly was tired of being called a bitch, so she was hanging out with some of her girlfriends. Jesse was alone, and the safest place to be alone at St. Gregory's was the library. Jesse went inside the school and headed straight for it. On his way there, he noticed a young man and woman standing behind a table covered in brochures and forms. They were wearing military uniforms, and their berets were fitted perfectly. There were posters on the wall behind them with pictures of airplanes and ships and tanks.

Because all the boys and girls were smiling in the shots, and because Jesse wasn't, he picked up a brochure and liked some of things he read:

Cadets offer you challenges, friendship, and adventure! It's an opportunity to expand your horizons, contribute to your community, and make friends for life.

When his mother got home from work that evening, he asked her if he could join.

She said she would talk it over with his father, which was her way of saying yes.

Jesse told Ryan about it later that night. Ryan liked what he heard and told Jesse that he didn't think his father would have any objections. "He'd probably be happy to see me go away for two months."

He walked into the living room and took one last look around. His set his eyes on the school photos that his mother had framed and hung on the wall above the couch that he slept on each morning after seeing his parents off to work.

Grade seven had been the year of the great scourge, when acne changed his life forever and people couldn't stop paying attention to him. He stood in front of the last photo that wasn't digitally altered—his grade six picture. He wanted to remind himself what life was like before acne.

Jesse could see his reflection in the glass of the picture frame. The once-clear skin in the photo was now covered in acne. There was no getting away from it. Jesse walked into the kitchen, where his mother was washing the dishes.

"Mom, did Dr. Sheffield get back to you about the acne medication?"

"Jesse, I told you! That stuff is for the worst-case scenario."

"Mom, I've tried almost everything and nothing has worked. Please call him soon and find out. Okay?"

The side effects of this new medication were harsh, and Mary told Dr. Sheffield that she wanted some time to think about it. He handed her the consent form that she would have to sign before he could prescribe the medication and went on to explain the waiver:

"Jesse must stop using the product if any of the following side effects occur: sad feelings or crying spells; loss of interest in his usual activities; changes in his normal sleep pattern; or if he becomes more irritable than usual."

Jesse told his mother that he could handle those side effects and that she had nothing to worry about. "Those things are normal for a teenager to go through, anyway. Maybe everyone in school is on the stuff and that's why they act the way they do!"

Watching her mull over the situation, Jesse could see that she wasn't convinced.

"I'm still not comfortable with the idea, Jesse." She wished her son wouldn't worry so much about what other people thought about his appearance. She dried her hands with a dishcloth and walked over to her son. "Listen, honey. The fresh air this summer will do your skin some good. Go to camp, fly in a plane, and you'll see how none of that stuff matters anymore. You graduated! And besides, your mother thinks you're beautiful!"

"You don't count," Jesse sulked.

"I used to."

Parents weren't allowed to drive their kids directly to the base, so they said their goodbyes from the mall, where two Greyhound buses waited to take the 983 Blue Jay Squadron to flight camp.

Parents took pictures, hugged their kids, and gave some final instructions:

"If you need anything, you call me."

"Don't forget to take your medication."

"Behave yourself."

"Make us proud, son!"

Jesse's mother wanted to take a picture. She had him stand by the bus and told him to smile. Standing there, Jesse couldn't help but be reminded of his first day of school, but he didn't want to think of school. Instead, he wondered what it was about the word cheese that worked so well for pictures.

"Say cheese," yelled his mother.

By the time Jesse finally got settled, the bus was full. The boy beside him shuffled nervously in his seat. He was heavy-set and was breathing rather sloppily. He was wearing a t-shirt far too small for someone his size. His face was covered in sweat, and when he leaned over Jesse to say goodbye to his parents, Jesse felt the boy's clammy skin against his arm.

The engine started. The bus roared to life.

Jesse looked out at his mother and smiled. He didn't have to see a tear to know that she was crying.

The boys on the bus passed the time with nervous chatter. Some played videogames, while others read comics and flipped through magazines. The boy beside Jesse didn't say much; he was too busy eating a bag of Oreo cookies. Jesse looked out the window and counted the planes that passed overhead.

When the bus turned into the camp entrance, all chatter ceased. Faces pressed up against the window. Some couldn't wait to get off the bus, and a few wished they didn't have to. Jesse's heart was racing. He looked out at the planes and the runway that only stopped at the horizon. The bus followed the runway, and Jesse imagined that it was plane ready for flight.

Each recruit was assigned a dorm and bunk number. Jesse was the first to enter Dorm A. He set his bags down on his designated bed and was happy that it was the bottom bunk. He walked over to the window and surveyed the base.

The dormitories reminded Jesse of the portables at school, only much bigger. There were eight of them. To the left was the runway, and to the right, a flat stretch of land. Jesse watched all the recruits carrying their wares, hunched over like old men herding sheep. He turned from the window when he heard voices.

Jesse saw the boy who sat beside him on the bus walk in and look for his bunk. Jesse hoped it wasn't going to be the one above him. But Jesse's hope was an invitation—the boy walked right up to Jesse's bunk and threw his bags on the top bed.

"Looks like we're bunk mates!"

When Jesse was finished unpacking, he sat on the edge of his bed and waited for something to happen. He was watching his squadron put their things together when a smell made him gasp. He turned his head and was looking at his bunkmate's naked feet.

The boy leaned over and offered him an Oreo. "I'm Derwin."

When everyone was settled and unpacked, the Warrant Officer informed them that the rest of the day was to do whatever they felt like doing, but "after dinner, there's an important meeting in the gym. Don't be late!"

One of the boys had heard that there was a river just on the other side of the runway; they packed up their towels and sunscreen and raced to see who would get there first.

Jesse's leg was feeling a little tense, and Derwin was out of breath. They walked and talked. Derwin was going into grade nine, and his father thought it would be a good idea for him to get in shape. "He told me that if I stayed fat, I would never get married and that I would die before my time." Derwin laughed and swallowed another Oreo.

Jesse didn't find it funny.

When they got to the river, the other boys in the squadron were already in the water. Jesse was excited. "Let's go!"

Derwin sat down in the grass and shook his head. "Nah, you go ahead. I don't like to swim."

Jesse could see from the tan lines on his arms that Derwin didn't like to take off his shirt. Jesse sat down and kept him company.

After their swim, the boys sat in the afternoon sun and talked.

Sam missed his dog, and Jonathan wanted an ice cream sandwich. Some of the older guys talked about high school.

Jesse told them he was starting grade nine.

"I don't envy you! I wouldn't want to go through that shit again!"

Jesse didn't ask what shit he was referring to—he had a pretty good idea already. He listened to the others talk amongst themselves and couldn't get it out of his head that they were all here, because they didn't want to be somewhere else: Sam had a big, crooked nose; Jonathan was short; Derwin was overweight; Jesse had acne.

Jesse noticed these things about other people because for so long people were noticing him. He remembered a comic that he read in grade three, where a fat cat hung out with fatter cats so that he could look thinner. It stuck with Jesse because, one day, after being told that he was nasty looking, he set out to look for someone ugly to hang out with before realizing what a ridiculous idea it had been. But he couldn't deny the fact that, when he hung out with people like Sam and Derwin, it made him feel a little bit better about his own appearance.

Later that evening, the squadron members gathered in the meeting hall. Jesse was a little nervous, so he took a seat beside Derwin who was sitting by himself and playing with an Oreo cookie.

A man in uniform stood up from his chair and took the microphone from the stand. "Good evening, everyone! I am your squadron leader, Colonel Reid, and I want to spend the next few minutes discussing a few things with you."

He spoke with such authority that Jesse was afraid to take his eyes off of him.

Colonel Reid outlined the uniform policy and reiterated how important it was for them to be in full uniform at all times. "Our uniform separates us from the rest of the community. It reminds people of who we are and, more importantly, it reminds you of who you are and the team that you are part of. Do the uniform proud. Be in full uniform at all times."

He reviewed the code of conduct and listed the punishments for various offenses. He put up an overhead that outlined the cadets' daily routines and schedules.

There were a lot of things to remember, and Jesse had a difficult time taking it all in. He realized that he had forgotten to take his Ritalin and hoped the Colonel would tell them when they were going to fly. The Colonel took a seat without answering Jesse's question.

Another senior officer stood up, introduced himself to the squadron, and reviewed all the rules, including who should be saluted and how persons of ranks should be addressed. He then told them about a program that Jesse wished they had had in elementary school. "We have what's known as the

Cadet Harassment and Abuse Prevention program, referred to as CHAP around here. This program provides you with an awareness of both your rights and your responsibilities in regards to harassment and abuse. We will teach you how to recognize inappropriate kinds of behaviour and what action should be taken in the event of such a case. CHAP addresses current issues and ensures that this program, which you all have signed up for, remains cutting-edge in terms of providing a safe and healthy environment in which young people can develop as strong and effective citizens. But I will warn you, if any of these rules are broken, your entire squadron will be punished and you will not be allowed to fly in two weeks."

There it was. It was music to Jesse's ears. In two weeks he'd be up in a plane, as long he didn't get into any trouble.

"Before we let you go, I want to mention one more thing. We want to equip each of you with important knowledge that you can incorporate into all facets of your life. Being able to recognize inappropriate behaviour and knowing what to do about it will help you establish yourself as a leader—whether it's in a classroom, on the sports field, or at a party with friends."

Jesse listened attentively and realized that he was here for two reasons: to fly planes and to learn how to survive.

"Are there any questions?"

Jesse saw a hand shoot up, somewhere near the front row.

"Sir? What's a facet?"

The squadron members laughed, then cowered under the Colonel's scornful gaze.

Jesse had no idea how much work went into being a pilot. The first week was spent marching and running drills under the unrelenting sun. He was having a difficult time with the marching. His knee hurt, so Jesse had to sit out a few of the activities to rest it.

One night, after taking a shower, he noticed a bump beginning to swell on his left knee. He was concerned, not for his health, but for his chance to fly in the plane. In order to fly, they had to complete basic training. So, just like he had done throughout elementary school, Jesse tried to show how little he hurt and carried on with the task.

Derwin wasn't as convincing.

On Tuesday he passed out from heat exhaustion, and on Thursday he threw up while trying to make it through the obstacle course.

It was a tough two weeks, having to always march in uniform; but Jesse was too close to the end, too close to getting his chance to finally fly, to give up early. He sucked up the pain and marched along. *"Left, right, left, right!"*

As the days passed and the sun scorched everything within its reach, Jesse couldn't help but notice how things were changing inside the dormitories and out in the field.

Alliances were formed and rules broken—it wasn't long before summer camp started to look like elementary school all over again. Everything was becoming a competition, and the tension was high in the dorms.

It was Derwin that Jesse worried about. The squadron members laughed when he ran his drills and teased him when he didn't shower at the same time as everybody else. Jesse spent his free time keeping Derwin company—he knew what it was like to be alone with so many people around. They played cards and read comics and sometimes went for long walks and talks.

The night before they were set to go up in the gliders, Jesse and Derwin sat on the picnic table outside the entrance to the dorm. They were playing poker, and there were fourteen Oreos in the pot.

Jesse could see how badly Derwin wanted to win the pot, so he folded his pocket aces and conceded the winnings to his friend.

As Derwin gathered his bounty, Jesse got up from the table. "I'm going to call my parents!" Jesse had thought about his mother a lot over the past two weeks, and he was beginning to really miss her.

Jesse inserted the quarter into the slot and hurriedly dialed his home number. After four rings the answering machine picked up.

"Shit!" Jesse spit out. Then, "Hi, guys. It's me. Things are good, and tomorrow they'll be even better: we finally get to go up in the gliders! I can't wait. Please say hello to Holly for me, and I hope that you're still not smoking. I love you guys. I'll call you after we land tomorrow." Jesse hung up the phone and decided he'd go to bed early—the sooner he slept, the earlier today ended and tomorrow began.

When he came out into the clearing, Derwin was no longer at the table. Jesse looked around, but saw and heard nothing. The silence sent a chill up his spine. Was everyone in bed already?

He walked past the picnic table and stopped in his tracks.

Derwin's cookies were still on the table. Jesse was about to pick them up, but he was startled by a strange sound.

He tiptoed back into the dorm. Three or four of the squadron members were sleeping, but all the other bunks were empty. Where was everybody?

Jesse heard a noise from the washroom.

"Shhhhhhh!"

Jesse slowly approached the bathroom door. He pressed his ear up against it, and heard feet shuffling back and forth. There were a few chuckling noises and a muffled sound that Jesse couldn't make sense of.

When he opened the door, he realized that what he had heard was Derwin trying to scream, but his mouth was taped with duct tape and he was lying in the bathtub.

He squiggled and squirmed while the others looked down at him and laughed.

Jesse looked around at the other squadron members. Their faces were different from the day they first met and swam in the river. They had a look that Jesse recognized all too well, for it was the same look that Martin and Rudy had down by the pond when Jesse was supposed to have been too sick to go to school.

He was quickly reminded of the trouble at school, and he wondered if there was any place on earth where this sort of thing didn't happen.

Jesse stared at Derwin, who was now crying and trying to push himself erect. Jesse took a step forward, but was pulled back and spun around.

"Oww!" Jesse felt something go pop in his left knee.

It was Jonathan, the guy who craved an ice cream sandwich down by the pond when they used to be all friends.

Jonathan leaned into Jesse. "Leave him alone! He can get up on his own."

Jesse looked away and tried to walk around him, but Sam blocked his way and pointed his finger at Jesse. "If you tell anyone about this, the whole squadron'll be fucked up. And you know what that means, right?"

He had no chance of making it past them. Jesse nodded and turned his back on his friend. "Yeah, we won't be able to fly tomorrow. I get it!"

Jesse was startled when his bunk began to shake in the middle of the night. He thought it was Derwin getting back into bed, but when he opened his eyes, he could see the impression of Derwin's body through the mattress. He was already in bed, and he was sobbing.

There was an awkward quiet in the dormitory the next morning. Some of the squadron members were whispering to one another and pointing at Derwin. Jesse packed up his day bag and put Elly's glasses into his shirt pocket, trying to forget about the night before. He wanted to say something to Derwin, but didn't.

They ate their breakfast in silence, until Derwin looked over at Jesse.

"Jesse, I don't want you to say anything. Okay?" Derwin looked away. "I don't want them to get even madder at me if we can't go out and fly today." In a small way, Jesse was glad that Derwin didn't want him to say anything, but he couldn't help but feel a little guilty.

Only two squadron members could go up in a glider at a time. Jesse and Derwin were partners. Derwin sat quietly as Jesse watched each plane start up and take off down the runway. The planes were much smaller than Jesse imagined, but the size of the plane did nothing to damper his enthusiasm to get up into the air.

When it was their turn for takeoff, Jesse could barely contain himself. He felt as if he was walking on clouds as he boarded the plane. After buckling his seatbelt, Jesse took a deep breath. He listened attentively to the roar of the engine and waited for it to make its way down the runway. The plane ascended into the sky and, for the first time in his life, Jesse knew what it was like to fly.

He pressed his face up against the window and watched the clouds and the birds pass by as the glider tilted from one side to the other.

He was flying and felt like crying, and he imagined that it felt the same way for an angel. He wondered if his parents were outside trying to catch a glimpse of their son up in the air.

It was the most incredible thing Jesse had ever experienced. It was one thing to see them landing or hanging from a string, but it was something else entirely to be inside of one, so high up off the ground. He secretly wished that he could be off the ground for good.

When the plane began to descend, he vowed to work even harder at school so that he'd get his chance to be a pilot, so that it could be him that was in control, taking people wherever they wanted to go and away from the place where they no longer wanted to be.

He thought about Ryan and couldn't wait to tell him about this. He thought about Elly for a second and then he remembered the sunglasses. He took them out of his jacket pocket and pretended that he wasn't a member of the 983 Blue Jay Squadron; instead, he was Maverick, a member of *Top Gun,* on his way to be being the best pilot to ever fly a plane.

He may have graduated from grade eight, but he felt that this was his real graduation. At 13 years of age, Jesse had realized a dream.

When the plane came to a stop, Jesse could barely contain himself. His heart was racing and he already looked forward to the next trip up. Jesse undid his seatbelt and looked over at Derwin.

"That was awesome, man!"

Derwin didn't seem all that impressed. He turned away from Jesse and struggled to get out of his seat.

Jesse didn't want to get off the plane. He took one last look around and couldn't wait to fly one on his own. He had one foot out the door when he realized that he had forgotten his sunglasses.

He was halfway into his step back when he felt his knee twist and give way. Jesse fell to the ground, held his knee, and called out for his mother.

CHAPTER SEVEN

He hoped his accident was just a dream. If he closed his eyes for a few seconds, maybe, just maybe, when he opened them, he'd be back on the bottom bunk, listening to Derwin cry and waiting for his next chance to fly. But when he opened his eyes, the only thing he saw was a plastic plane.

Jesse sighed. He wondered when a good day would be followed by a good week and an even better month, rather than going to bed happy and waking up sad.

Jesse lifted himself out of bed and limped downstairs so that he could spend some time with his parents before they left for work. His father put down the newspaper.

"How's the knee, son?"

"Not bad," Jesse lied. He sat down beside his mother and kissed her on the cheek. She smiled and put her hand on his knee.

"I'm going to make an appointment with Dr. Sheffield for tomorrow, Jesse. In the meantime, I want you to rest and stay off your leg."

Jesse looked at his mother. "Mom, how can I stay off my leg? There's six weeks of summer left and no one is around. I'm going to have to find something to do."

"Well, whatever you do, make sure it isn't too stressful on your leg."

Jesse looked down at his knee.

His mother could see how disappointed he was. "Honey, at least you got a chance to fly! There'll always be next summer, baby."

"Yeah, next summer," Jesse lamented.

After his parents left for work, Jesse lay on the couch and tried to get used to the silence. The house was empty; Jesse was alone, the same way he was alone when he pretended to be sick so he didn't have to go to school. Only this time he wasn't pretending—there was no school to go to.

He couldn't get the look of Derwin's eyes out of his head. He heard the sound of his crying as if Jesse was still on the bunk beneath him. But he wasn't. Jesse was on his couch, eating a Chips Ahoy cookie because he couldn't stand the sight of the Oreos.

"I didn't even have a chance to say goodbye to him," Jesse spoke out loud, and he felt guilty for not reporting the incident.

He remembered how they all sat in the gymnasium and listened to the Colonel promise them a healthy and safe environment. Jesse felt betrayed. He had hoped Cadets was going to be different from school; it wasn't. Cadets and school. Winners and losers. Survivors and victims.

He got up from the couch and drew back the blinds of the screen door. He could see that the fish were happy and the squirrels were content. Jesse looked at the birds nervously pacing on top of the fence, looking as if they needed a place to call home. He decided to build a birdhouse.

Jesse liked working with wood. His father still had the small block of wood with the thirty-one nails that were supposed to be candles. Jesse made it in grade three and gave it to his father on his birthday. Jesse's father pretended to blow out the candles and thanked his son for the cake.

Jesse called for Holly and headed to the garage to begin work on his new summer project.

Scanning all the tools and supplies, Jesse stood with his hands on his waist. He didn't know where to begin. He decided to start from scratch and hope for the best.

After about an hour, he was getting tired and decided to take a break. He walked to the side of the house to turn on the water. He soaked the back of his neck, running some of the cool water over his face and through his hair.

Jesse stood at the entrance of the garage and looked up and down his street. He couldn't help but notice how quiet it was. The street used to be full of kids playing hide-and-seek, jump rope, soccer, baseball, and sometimes soccer-baseball.

He was about to get back to work, when he was startled by the sound of a door slamming shut. Jesse looked out across the street and watched Mr. George step gingerly into his yard and pick up a shovel.

The Georges were the oldest people in the neighbourhood. Over the years, Jesse learned that they had each been married three times before meeting each other, and each time they had outlived their spouses.

Mrs. George came outside and put something small into her husband's hand, then passed him a glass of water.

Jesse figured they were pills and wondered what was wrong with him.

"Old age, I guess," Jesse figured. He felt sorry for the old man because he was starting to understand how he felt.

Mrs. George took the glass from her husband and turned to go back into the house. Before she shut the door, she turned back to yell, "Now honey, don't work yourself too hard! You know you have bad knees!"

Jesse watched Mr. George limp through his garden, trying and keep his balance as he bent down and pulled out a weed.

He couldn't believe that this old man, who was popping pills and looking as if he were going to fall apart, was the same man they had all feared as children.

Jesse remembered the night, while playing street hockey with Ryan and a few friends, his slap shot missed the net and smacked right into the passenger door of Mr. George's car. They all stood still, hoping that they're lives weren't about to come to an end, as they saw the door of the house open and the old man come outside.

"By Jesus, if you don't watch out for my car the Devil will eat your soul!"

But over time, instead of running for their lives, they all stood and mocked the old man until he threw up his hands in disgust and slammed the door on his way back inside the house. He was old, and young people had no time for old people.

Jesse decided he had done enough work for the day. He was in the middle of putting the tools away when he heard a cough behind him and turned around.

It was Mr. George, looking as if he would fall over at any minute.

"Excuse me, son." Mr. George coughed again, then wiped the phlegm from his lips with the palm of his hand. "Jesse, right?"

Jesse nodded.

"I've heard your name a thousand times." Mr. George was silent; it looked to Jesse like he was trying to remember the first time he had heard it. "Listen, do you think you could give me a hand for a second? My knee is killing me. I'm not as strong as I used to be I'm afraid."

Jesse's leg was also hurting, but not so much that he couldn't help an old man with his chores.

Wherever Mr. George pointed, Jesse bent down and pulled out the weeds. He spread the woodchips, and Mr. George told him where he could find another bag of fertilizer. Jesse was thankful when Mrs. George came out with egg salad sandwiches and a pitcher of lemonade. His knee was starting to really throb, and he needed the break.

Mr. George liked to talk, and, in some small way, Jesse was happy to be listening. He was a good storyteller. The only time he stopped talking was when a plane passed by overhead. "You know, son, I used to fly planes!"

"Really?" Jesse asked, extending the invitation that Mr. George had been hoping for.

He told Jesse that he had been in the RAF during World War II, a pilot, fighting against the worst tyrant in history. He told Jesse that his plane had been hit in an air-fight over Austria, and a piece of a glass from the accident had punctured his eardrum. "I knew I would never hear out of it again."

Jesse felt sorry for the old man.

"Ah, don't worry, Jesse. I can still hear out of the other one, even though I like to pretend sometimes that I can't! It really irks the old lady." Mr. George nodded his head in the direction of the house and put his finger up to his mouth to signal it was he and Jesse's little secret.

Jesse looked at the old man and suddenly felt guilty. He thought about all the times they made fun of him for how slow he drove his car, and how funny it was that he walked with a limp. Jesse had no idea that they were making fun of a real hero.

"How come you went into the war, Mr. George?"

Mr. George looked at him with the eyes of a hero, instead of an old man.

"I didn't like what Hitler was doing to the Jews. Hitler wanted a uniform Germany. He wanted everybody to look alike and act alike, and he did his best to terrorize those

81

people that didn't. I went into the war because I wanted to help make the world a safer place for everybody, Jesse."

Mr. George turned his neck as much as he could toward the house and yelled, "Barbara! Bring out the picture, dear," as if there was only one picture in the entire house.

Mrs. George returned a few moments later with the picture and set it down in front of her husband, shaking her head as she walked back into the house. "How come you don't show off our wedding picture like you do this one?"

Mr. George winked at Jesse and smiled.

Jesse liked the photo. It was of Mr. George, only he was much younger, standing in front of an airplane with his left hand on his hip and his right hand holding his helmet. The word *Silk* was stenciled under the window of the cockpit.

"Was Silk your nickname, Mr. George?" Jesse asked.

"Captain said I flew I like silk, and the name stuck!"

"I like it!" Jesse's mind was awash with nicknames for the plane he was hoping to fly one of these days. He looked at Mr. George and smiled. "I want to be a pilot, too."

Over dinner that night, Jesse couldn't help but think about the stories that Mr. George had told him about World War II. Jesse decided he wanted to be a fighter pilot, because he liked the idea of helping people.

"Mom, do you think I'll be able to go back to Cadets next summer?" Jesse asked as he helped his mother clean up the table.

"Oh my God! I can't believe I forgot to tell you. I'm getting so old!"

She turned the faucet off and grabbed a dishcloth to dry her hands.

"They called me at work today to see how you were doing. They said as long as your knee is good, they would love to have you back next year!"

Relieved, Jesse told his mother he wanted to be fighter pilot.

"You can do whatever you want, baby. I just want you to take it easy. You know you have a bad knee!"

Jesse sighed; Mrs. George had said that exact same thing to her husband earlier that afternoon.

The next day, he sat across from Dr. Sheffield and listened to him diagnose Jesse with a disease he could barely pronounce.

"Jesse, you have what's known as Osgood Schlatter's disease. It's a disease that primarily affects boys under the age of 16 and, in particular, those who are involved in sports or just like to run around a lot. Your mother tells me that you were running drills and marching a lot this summer?"

To Jesse, it was beginning to feel like years ago.

"Now, it may persist until you stop growing. There's nothing we can really do right now other than to prescribe plenty of rest. In a month, we'll be fitting you in a cast."

Jesse looked at his mom desperately. "But getting a cast next month means I'll be wearing a cast in high school!"

He didn't think that a cast was a particularly hot fashion item. His mother could only offer a sympathetic smile. "Is the cast absolutely necessary, Dr. Sheffield?" she asked on her son's behalf.

"I'm afraid so. It'll force the knee to rest and heal much more quickly. It'll only be for a month. For now, I want you to follow the RICE procedure: rest, ice, compression, and elevation."

Jesse got up from the chair and shook Dr. Sheffield's hand without looking at him or thanking him. "It's only for a month, Jesse, " Dr. Sheffield tried to reassure him.

The fact that it was only for a month did nothing to assuage his fears. If high school was going to be anything like elementary school, he was going to need maximum mobility.

With only a week to go until school began, Jesse had yet to hear from Ryan. He had called him a few times and left a few messages, but his calls were never returned. Just when Jesse was beginning to think that he might not see Ryan at all, he unexpectedly showed up one night after dinner and told Jesse that he wanted to talk to him about something.

Before Ryan could say what was on his mind, Jesse figured that it had something to do with Ryan's appearance because, looking at him for the first time in six weeks, he could barely recognize his best friend.

His hair was dyed blonde and he was wearing clothes that someone his age shouldn't have been able to afford. "What did your dad say about the nose ring, man?"

"He didn't care as long as I paid for it. It's not like he pays much attention to me anyway."

They walked into the living room and threw themselves on the couch. Ryan asked about the Cadets and tried to make it look as if he was paying attention. Jesse could tell that something was on his mind and that it didn't have anything to do with Cadets or plane rides.

"What's up, Ryan?"

A phone rang.

Ryan reached into his pocket and pulled out his cell.

"Man, those things are annoying!" Jesse spit out. "I didn't know you had a cell phone!"

"It's the *bling-bling*, man! Hold on a sec." Ryan put his finger into his ear and answered his phone, "Yo!"

Jesse watched Ryan talk and felt like a lot more was changing about him besides his physical appearance.

"Sorry about that, man. That was a guy from work. We're going out tonight. Wanna come?"

"I can't. My knee is a mess and have to try and stay off it."

Jesse told him about his knee and how he was going to have to wear a cast in high school. He admitted that it frightened him.

"That's what I wanted to talk to you about. Jesse, I want us to try and do things differently this year."

"What do you mean?"

"I mean, I don't want us to be on the defensive all through high school. I don't want us to be afraid to do things or to go places. I don't want to be afraid of sitting in someone's spot in the cafeteria or a classroom. I'm sick of that shit, man! And the only way for us to avoid that is to set the right tone from the very first day. Let's let people know that we're not afraid of them."

Jesse looked over at Ryan and could see that he had already been on the offensive for some time.

He reminded Jesse of Martin and Rudy and their gang, with their daily efforts to look cool and stay cool. Jesse could see that they had worked over his best friend to the point that he wanted to be just like them: always on the prowl, always on the attack.

Ryan reached into his back pocket. The last time Jesse had seen Ryan reach into his pocket he had pulled out a joint. This time it was a butterfly knife.

The only knives Jesse handled were the knives in his dreams. "What am I gonna do with that?" he asked.

"Go on the offensive, man! It's not like you have to use it."

"If I won't have to use it, why the hell do I need it?"

"If someone bugs you, just pull your shirt to the side and let them see it there. Set the tone. Jesse, I spent a lot of time with my brother this summer and he said if he could do it again, he would do it with one of these."

Jesse looked at the knife in his best friend's hand. It was the same hand that Ryan used to throw a tennis ball with, a Frisbee with; the same hand Jesse slapped for a high-five after scoring another goal.

Jesse shrugged his shoulders.

"Fine, don't take it. But I'm telling you, you better be ready! I know I'm tired of watching other people being cool. I want people to look at me for something other than what I'm being picked on or made fun of for!"

Ryan was almost of breath, and the harder he breathed, the more Jesse could smell the pot. "It's there for the taking, Jesse—you just have to take it." Ryan looked down at the knife as if he wished he never had to take it.

Jesse smirked. "What's so cool about being cool anyway?"

"You just don't get it, Jesse. You don't get it!"

"Get what?"

Ryan opened his mouth but his cell phone rang again.

"Yo!" Ryan stood and waved goodbye while talking to whoever was on the line. Jesse watched him limp out of his house, down the driveway, and into the street. Ryan looked around and hoped that someone was watching him be tough.

Jesse went back to the living room, threw himself on the couch, lifted his knee and set his foot atop the coffee table. The smell of pot lingered, and Jesse could still hear Ryan's voice.

"It's there for the taking, man—you just have to take it!"

He turned on the television and watched the *Wanna be a Rock Star* marathon on MTV, where people tried so hard to be someone else, to feel like someone else besides themselves, even if only for a day.

"Maybe Ryan's right. Maybe I could do a better job of trying to fit in."

Jesse thought about all the things that Ryan had said, but he was still not convinced that the knife was necessary.

When his mother got home from work that night he asked her if he could get an earring.

"What do you want an earring for, Jesse?"

"I just think it'll look good, Ma!"

Mary turned and looked at her son. "Jesse, you don't need an earring to look good."

"I know, Ma, I know. So, can I get one?"

A few days later, Jesse decided he needed a cell phone and asked his mother over supper if he could have one. "It'll be good for high school, Ma. You know—in case anything happens." He felt a little guilty about playing the safety card, but surmised that there was no room for guilt when a person went on the offensive. If he was going to have to wear a cast, at least he could try and look cool in one. If he wasn't going to carry a knife around, he could at least take a stab at fitting in.

A few days before the start of school Jesse's mother took him downtown to pick up his school uniform.

Jesse had heard that St. Elizabeth's had a strict uniform policy. A navy blue sweater with the school motto: *Commitment, Justice, Love, and Peace.* Pants had to be grey, and their white dress shirts were not allowed to have any logos on them. Jesse tried on a few sweaters, a couple of cardigans, and a couple pairs of pants, and walked out of the place with his high school uniform.

Elly returned from the cottage the day before high school was set to begin.

She smiled from ear to ear when she walked up to the door and saw Jesse for the first time in nearly eight weeks. "Hey, man! I love the earring! It looks hot!"

Jesse smiled and blushed and hugged her. It didn't take long for Jesse to notice just how much Elly was changing as well.

Her hair was streaked with red highlights, her nails were painted red. Her teeth were as white as Jesse's dress shirt, and she was more beautiful than Jesse could have ever imagined. He felt better about being on the offensive and was happy to be keeping pace with everyone else, but he still wished that Elly would be going to school with him tomorrow.

They sat in silence for a few moments before Elly got up, straightened her skirt, and reached out for Jesse's hand as if she was about to ask him to dance.

"Well, babe, I guess this it. High school tomorrow!" Elly squeezed Jesse's hand. Jesse wished he could hold onto it forever.

Before calling it a night, Jesse put on his uniform one last time and stood in front of the mirror. He felt as if he was looking at himself for the first time in a long time: a new earring, a new uniform, and a new cell phone—a new look. But then he caught a glimpse of his acne, thought about his knee and the cast he was going to have to wear for a month, and about Ryan's knife and Elly's scholarship, and about Derwin's Oreos and deaf Mr. George, and about flying for the first time. So much had happened, so much had changed in two months, that he was feeling more tired than he should have been after a long holiday. He looked at himself in the mirror one last time and, for a second, didn't recognize the boy looking back at him.

CHAPTER EIGHT

Jesse wasn't sure if he had slept or not. The last time he looked at the clock it was 4:37 a.m. Now it was 6:30 a.m., and it was time for Jesse to get up. The nauseous feeling in his stomach reminded him of what day it was, and he wished he didn't have to get out of bed. It was the first day of school all over again. Jesse could only hope and pray that high school was going to be different.

"Good morning, my little gift," his mother called up to him from the stairs. "Time for another first day of school!"

"I'll be downstairs in a minute, Mom." He dragged himself out of bed and took his uniform off the back of his door. He laid it out on his bed and looked at the ensemble. He was still hopeful that the uniform might help even up the odds.

He picked up the white dress shirt and handled it as if it were made of crystal. It was the cleanest shirt he had ever seen, and he was careful when he put it on. He did up the buttons from the bottom up, then buttoned his sleeves and checked his collar. He stepped into his grey dress pants and pulled them over the white shirt. He ran a belt through the loops and ran his hands over his pants to flatten out any creases. He put on his grey socks and tied up his new size-thirteen sneakers.

He walked over to his bed and picked up his sweater. He put his arms into the sleeves and pulled the sweater over his chest and, for the first time, was in full uniform. Jesse anxiously tugged at his sweater and tried to straighten out another crease in his pants.

"Well? Whad'ya think, Holly?" Holly wagged her tail and tried to jump on him.

"No, Holly! I'm not going to school with dog hair all over me!" Jesse pushed her away and walked over to the window. He looked over at the cross that marked his destination like the letter X on a map. Jesse took a breath.

He brushed his teeth, applied gel to his new hairstyle, freshened himself with some cologne, and shut the lights before he had a chance to get a good look at his face. His morning was off to a good start and he didn't want to jeopardize it by catching a glimpse of his acne.

Jesse gathered his things: binders, pens, and pencils. He picked up his new cell phone from his desk and saw a message from Elly: *Good luck, buddy!*

His parents didn't hear him tiptoeing down the stairs, so their backs were turned when he walked into the dining room where they were having coffee.

Jesse cleared his throat to get their attention.

"Well?" Jesse asked, putting his hands in his pockets and feeling a little shy.

His mother put down her mug and turned around, instantly remembering that first day of kindergarten. "Oh, baby! You look absolutely beautiful!"

She put her hands up to her mouth and was proud of her son.

His father looked up from the paper and nodded and winked. "The girls'll be all over you boy!"

Mary elbowed her husband and got up to hug her son. Taking a step back to get a better look at him, she looked

Jesse up and down and wept. "I am so proud of you, my little gift!"

Jesse tugged at his sweater and shifted from one leg to the other. "I feel like a gift, wrapped up in this damn uniform! It feels awkward!"

"It's like shoes, honey. It'll take some time for you to work it in."

"Maybe I'm not supposed to go to St. Elizabeth's," he halfheartedly joked.

His mother pinched him.

"I'm just kidding!"

"Are you excited?" his father asked.

"More nervous than excited," Jessie replied, drying his sweaty palms on his pants.

His mom, who was still holding onto him, regained her composure and smiled. "Listen, if you need anything, you can always call me at work."

"I will, Ma." He picked up his bag, and his parents walked him to the door.

"Did you take your Ritalin?" his mother asked.

"No, not yet." Jesse thought it might be a good idea if he took the whole bottle with him to school, just in case he really needed it, so he had packed it in his bag with the rest of his things.

"Do you have your schedule?"

"In my pocket!"

"Well, it looks to me like you're all ready for high school."

"Yeah, it looks that way, doesn't it?" When he knelt down to pick up his bag, he felt a spasm in his knee and stood up straight with some difficulty.

"Let's just hope high school is ready for you, son!" his father proclaimed, and nudged his son at the shoulder.

Jesse kissed them both on the cheek and was turning to walk out the door when his mother told him to wait so that she could take a picture.

Jesse remembered Martin being jealous that his mother didn't take a picture of him on his first day of school. "Ma, let's not start high school the way we did elementary school." He didn't want to take any chances.

"Okay, baby."

Jesse was sorry that he had disappointed his mother, but it was the least he could do to try and protect himself. When he reached the driveway, Jesse saw a flash of light bounce off the window of the car. He turned around and smiled at his mother, who took another picture.

"I couldn't resist! It's for the *Book of Firsts*, baby."

Jesse knocked on Ryan's door and waited. To quell his anxiety, Jesse pulled his schedule out of his pocket and looked at it for the fifth time that morning—just to be safe.

He surveyed the room numbers and the time that each class would start. He was worried about the five minutes between each class, the five minutes when students swelled into the halls en masse.

"Looking good, loser!"

Jesse jumped. For a moment, he thought he was at school and not standing on his best friend's doorstep. He regained his composure and took a deep breath and looked at Ryan in his uniform. "Not looking so bad yourself, dude!"

"Yeah, right. C'mon, let's go." Ryan locked the door and followed Jesse to the sidewalk.

As they walked, Jesse counted planes and Ryan fidgeted with something in his back pocket. They marched toward the end of the street feeling that once they reached it, nothing would ever be the same.

Ryan looked over at Jesse. "Hey, you gonna say something?"

"Sorry, man."

"What are you doing anyway?"

"Counting planes."

"Are you nervous or something?" Ryan hoped that he was.

"No," Jesse lied.

"Then what are you counting planes for?"

"What's wrong with counting planes? You used to count planes with me, man!"

"Yeah, but we also thought we could throw a tennis ball up to God," Ryan sniped back, waving his hand as if trying to sweep the past behind him. They were high school students, one step closer to being adults, and Ryan didn't have time for God or planes.

When they reached the intersection across the street from the school, Jesse and Ryan stopped. Jesse looked at the place that would house the drama of his life for the next four years. He had heard so much about high school, seen too many films about high school, and now he was about to begin his first day of high school. Crossing the street would be like crossing a border, stepping into an unknown world where everything was new and everyone was a stranger.

Ryan took a deep breath and felt for the knife that was tucked into his waistband. He remembered his brother's voice: *"If anyone picks on you, pull your cardigan back and hold it there long enough for them to see the handle. And don't worry—you won't have to use it. Just let the fuckers see it. It's just like in the movies!"*

Jesse looked over at Ryan. "What did you say?"

"Nothing."

"You said something about the movies, man!"

Jesse shifted his weight from one leg to the next, nervous, hoping the light would never turn green. He watched the fifth plane pass overhead and remembered his mothers words from so long ago: *"If you want to fly planes..."* It wasn't kindergarten anymore, but once again, his dream to fly sealed the deal.

There was a procession of cars pulling into the school parking lot, the drivers honking their horns and yelling at the students walking slow enough to make a point.

Every time a Honda Civic passed, the driver pressed the gas and let out a blast, and everybody's head would turn.

Ryan looked at all the cars and was envious. "I can't wait to get my license, man!"

"Punch buggy red!" Jesse shouted as if to remind himself that he was still thirteen and shouldn't be so afraid of school.

Ryan wasn't amused and looked around to see if anyone was looking. "Jesse! What the hell did I tell you about that childish shit?"

Jesse was sorry he had punched him, but forgot about it when he saw another plane flying overhead and counted six in his head.

The light turned green.

"It's a go, baby!" Ryan announced.

Jesse couldn't help but notice that Ryan was walking with a bit of a limp. The bulge in his back pocket told Jesse that Ryan was packing more than a lunch.

As he got closer to the school, Jesse heard nothing but the sounds of spitting, snorting, swearing, cursing, kissing, laughing, and whistling. "Yo, Yo . . . Holy shit—look at you . . . I love your hair . . . Sweet rims, man . . . Oh, she broke up with him last week . . . Ya, he got back with her two days ago . . . Did you hear . . . Did you see . . . Did you hear . . . Did you hear . . . "

Ryan elbowed Jesse who was listening to the racket.

"Hey, did you hear me? There's my friend from work. Let's go talk to him for a bit."

Jesse shook his head. "Nah, I don't want to be late for first period."

Ryan turned around and started to walk away. "Suit yourself. I'll catch up with you in fifth period, alright?"

Jesse watched his best friend leave, and he felt terribly alone.

He turned reluctantly and faced the entrance to school. He didn't know what to expect and was hesitant about walking in by himself. He turned around one last time to look over at Ryan, who was having a cigarette and telling a story that he must have been really exciting because he was jumping up and down between drags.

Jesse looked up at the crucifix engraved into the brick above the door and figured that his chances were better with Jesus than they were with Ryan. He opened the big, blue doors to his first day of high school, hoping he'd find heaven instead of hell.

The foyer was large and had a huge staircase that split in two directions up to the second floor. On the landing stood a statue of the Virgin Mary caressing her baby Jesus. Over her shoulder, Jesse could see a group of students pointing from the other side of the glass, checking out at all the new students and perhaps making fun of some of the old.

It was a much brighter place than Jesse had imagined. The centre of the roof was a skylight that looked to be the impression of a wedding cake. There were pictures of saints all around, and another crucifix stood in the middle of the foyer, a few feet in front of the stairs. No one was around it.

He didn't know whether to stand and wait for a familiar face or walk the halls on his own. He decided on the latter, because standing alone was such an un-cool thing for a teen to do. There were too many people, too many eyes watching, and Jesse's spine was tingling.

"This is why I wanted Elly here with me," Jesse muttered, hoping that no one saw him talking to himself.

The halls were congested with human traffic. People were moving in no particular direction and not looking to be in any rush. Jesse tried to stay alert, because he didn't want to be left behind on his first day of school.

Girls were looking into mirrors at their lockers, and some of the guys were looking at magazines and talking on their phones or taking pictures with their phones. Everyone seemed to be telling stories about their summers and all the things that they didn't really do. There were faces Jesse recognized, but a lot more that he didn't. Those he did know, he acknowledged with a "What's up!" and felt good about it each time.

He took out his schedule to make sure he was going in the right direction.

Room 117.

He caught a glimpse of Martin and Rudy looking more alike than ever in their uniforms. But something about them looked different to Jesse; somehow they seemed less threatening. Perhaps it was because of the number of students in the halls, or maybe it was because they blended in so well with everyone else. They were jumping up and down and banging their hands against the locker until a teacher walked by and stared them down. They no longer jumped or yelled, but they did give the teacher the finger behind his back and then took off down the hall.

Because Jesse was looking one way and walking in another, he didn't see where he was going and walked straight into someone's shoulder. Jesse prayed that it was someone he knew. It wasn't.

"Hey! Watch yourself, kid!"

He had never seen her before and didn't think this was going to be a particularly good first impression.

"Sorry. I'm sor—"

"You should be. Stupid niner!" She turned her back on Jesse like he wasn't even there.

Jesse walked away and hoped Room 117 was close by. When he found it, he found a seat in the back and took a very deep breath. He reached into his pocket and pulled out his bottle of Ritalin. Undoing the top, he swallowed two pills and didn't bother with water because he'd have to go back out into the halls to get some.

The girl he bumped into walked by his class. Jesse thought about hiding for a second, but realized where he was and gave his head a shake. "How did she know I was in grade nine, anyway?" he whispered to himself. He looked down at his desk and saw beads of sweat.

"Good morning, class. My name is Miss Simic..."

Jesse looked up and saw the prettiest teacher he had ever seen. Her hair was streaked with different colours, her clothes were funky, and she wore thick glasses—the kind that makes a person look smart.

She was young, and Jesse liked the way she smiled.

"I'm your grade nine religion teacher. After announcements, I'll be going over the course outline with you. Stand for the anthem and morning prayer, please."

Students threw back their chairs, banging them into the desks behind them—they weren't yet familiar with their new surroundings. After the Our Father and the national anthem, the principal came over the PA and asked all the students to sit and pay attention to the following announcements:

"Good morning everyone. My name is Principal Scully, and I would like to take this opportunity to welcome you back to St Elizabeth's. For those of you who are newly joining us, I would like to say welcome. Our school motto at St. Elizabeth's is 'Commitment, Justice, Love, and Peace.'"

Jesse sat attentively as Principal Scully reminded the students that, as long as they were in school, they were expected to be in full uniform.

"The school uniform is a very important part of who we are. It is what unites us as a family. It reminds us that we belong to a very special community, that we are all part of the same team, and that we all—you all—have an equal opportunity for success in your high school career."

Jesse couldn't help but think of the CHAP program at Cadets and how neither initiative applied to Derwin.

"Before I go, I want each and every one of you to know that my staff and I are going to do everything we can to make sure that you achieve your academic and personal goals throughout the year."

Before signing off, he repeated the school slogan and wished everyone a good day.

Miss Simic instructed the class to open up their notebooks. She walked around the room, distributing the course outline and making sure that the girl's kilts weren't too high and the boy's pants weren't too low.

"The title of the course is..."

She walked up the board and continued writing as she spoke.

"...B-e W-i-t-h M-e." Jesse picked up his pen and starting copying the note. Some of the boys shuffled in their seats and snickered. The boy in front of Jesse leaned over and whispered to his friend, "I'd be with her no problem, man!"

"Now, can anyone tell me who 'me' might be?" Miss Simic asked the class.

"You mean *me* is not *you*?" The boy in front of Jesse asked and looked around the class for approval. Most of the students were too nervous to laugh.

"No! 'Me' is not *me*," Miss Simic responded, shooting the boy a look that told him not to try it again.

"And please, put your hand up when you have an answer to a question!"

The class giggled. Jesse noticed two girls in the middle of the class pointing at a boy who was biting his nails and rocking in his seat. They looked at each other and tried to conceal their laughter by covering their mouths with their hands.

Miss Simic continued: "The 'me' I'm referring to here is Jesus—"

There was a collective groan.

"—and throughout the course, we are going to look at our relationship with him. But first we're going to take a look at ourselves. The first unit is called *Who Do I Want To Be?* We are going to examine the people you look up to and what that says about you and your relationship with Jesus."

History class may have only been seventy minutes in length, but to Jesse, it felt more like three years. Mr. Lima was the opposite of Miss Simic. He was much older, and he barely smiled. It was as if there was nothing about history worth smiling about.

He slurred his words, and his glasses kept falling down the bridge of his nose.

Jesse had almost fallen asleep a couple of times, and if it wasn't for Mr. Lima bumping into desks and sending things crashing to the floor, Jesse might have slept through the entire class.

From the back of the class, Jesse overheard two students crack jokes about the old man. He heard one of them wish that Mr. Lima would just die and get on with it.

Jesse was bored, but he wasn't mean.

He was happy to hear the bell that brought an end to history for the day.

It was time for lunch.

Jesse walked out into the halls and could see everyone decorating their lockers as if they were walls in their own rooms. They put up pictures, mirrors, a note pad, another mirror, decorating the one thing that they could call their own in high school. It was their main space—their real estate—and they decorated it as if their life depended on it.

Jesse was assigned locker 1109, and he was happy to find it was just outside his first period class. He thought about putting up a few pictures, but he certainly wasn't going to put up a mirror. Jesse set his bag down and searched for his lunch.

"Shit," Jesse spit out. "I forgot my lunch!" Jesse's stomach, as if to taunt him, growled. He checked his pockets to see how much money he had and headed reluctantly towards the cafeteria.

The cafeteria had tables that could be converted into benches and a stage against the back wall. The café was off to the left and on his right ran a glass wall, on the other side of which was the Hall of Heroes that students had to march through to get to the gym.

Students were playing dominoes, cards, and video games, and were listening to music through headphones. A few girls were singing up on the stage while a few guys clapped along.

Jesse recognized a few faces; people from elementary school sitting with the same people from elementary school, hoping that no one would notice that they hadn't made any new friends.

Jesse walked into the café and took his place at the end of the line.

He read over the menu and could see that it was pretty much the same as St. Gregory's: fried chicken and mashed potatoes, beef patties, hamburgers, fries, pop, rice in water, four-dollar tuna sandwiches, five-dollar salads, and half-price chocolate bars.

Jesse decided on the fried chicken with fries and wondered what he could get for dessert. He was looking over at the chocolate bars when he noticed the boy from religion class that wouldn't stop biting his nails.

He was shorter than Jesse by a couple of inches. His hair was unkempt, and he looked as if he was doing everything in his power to avoid making eye contact with anyone.

Jesse was just thinking that it might be a good idea to introduce himself, when he noticed a few students—three girls and one very big guy wearing his football jacket like a trophy—acting strangely nearby. Jesse saw the football player's eyes light up the moment the girls began pointing at the nail-biter. They were like the eyes of a lion that was ready to pounce on a zebra with three legs. Jesse watched the lion sneak up behind its prey, push the small boy from behind, and then look around to make sure that people were paying attention.

It was the same style as Rudy and Martin, and Jesse knew that the boy was in for it.

"Watch where you're going, geek!"

"But I wasn't going anywhere," the three-legged zebra replied.

"That's the point, buddy! I better not see you anywhere around school. My name's Billy, and these are my friends..." He made a sweeping gesture as if to suggest that everyone in the café was his friend. "If you know what's good for you, you'll remember my voice, avoid my face, and make sure that I don't see you around this year. Got it?" It sounded like a rehearsed speech.

Jesse paid for his food and followed the boy outside.

The bright sun blinded Jesse as he walked through the doors. He figured the boy couldn't have gone very far, and finally found him sitting with his back against the wall just outside the special-ed department.

Jesse walked over and introduced himself and could see that the boy was praying the rosary.

He looked up at Jesse and smiled.

"I'm Daniel," he said and motioned for Jesse to put down his tray and sit down. "You know, that guy was the first person to say anything to me today!"

Jesse looked at him and smiled. "Well, count me as the second."

He gave Daniel his fries, and they spent the rest of lunch eating in silence.

By the end of the day Jesse was swamped with homework, but he was feeling good about his first day of high school.

After squeezing all of his books into his backpack, he zipped up his bag and shut his locker.

"What's up, maaan?"

Jesse jumped. It was Ryan.

"Where you been? You skipped fifth period!"

"I've been around. Listen, I'm gonna hang around for a bit with some of these guys I met today. Do you wanna come?"

"I have way too much homework. Speaking of homework— what about you?"

"I'll do it eventually. Listen, I gotta run. I'll call you later!"

Jesse watched Ryan run away from him for the second time that day. He walked home by himself, but was happy that he got through his first day without too many problems. He had seen Martin and Rudy, but they hadn't seen him. He knew it would only be a matter of time, but Jesse wasn't too concerned. He had met a new friend and was beginning to feel that he was watching an old friend grow old. Jesse counted the planes that passed overhead as he walked, and he looked forward to flying again some day. He scoped out another plane until it disappeared from sight.

CHAPTER NINE

Sunday was Jesse's least favourite day of the week. Whether it was a Sunday that concluded a week of the school year, or a Sunday that ended another week in the summer, the mornings were saved for church and the afternoons for visiting family and friends.

But the Sunday that concluded the first week of grade nine was a good one. Jesse's parents may not have bought him a present, but they did bring him to the airport where they watched planes take off and land.

His mother packed a lunch, while his father filled the cooler with bottles of water and "just a couple of beers." He winked at Jesse and promised him a sip.

Between bites of tuna sandwiches and pickles and watching planes passing overhead, Jesse told his parents about his first week of school. They sat on the hood of the car drinking coffee and eating donuts, and he told them about Miss Simic and Daniel and lied about Ryan when his mother asked about him.

He told them that he passed a quiz and that he liked the food in the café.

"How's everything else going?" Jesse's mother asked.

Jesse assumed she was making reference to the bullying. He couldn't find any reason to suggest that high school was going to be much tougher than elementary school. There was the girl that he bumped into on his very first day, but he hadn't seen her the rest of the week and considered the matter closed. He thought about Daniel and how he left the café with no food, but that was Daniel, not him, so Jesse looked up at his mother and smiled.

"Everything's been good," Jesse said, glad he could speak truthfully.

He watched a 747 glide through the air as if by magic, reminding him of flying carpets and wizards and dragons from stories in kindergarten. They flew through the air at will, leaving the world below, soaring freely among the birds, clouds, and angels.

Jesse watched and remembered so vividly his first time up in the plane—how good it was to have his feet off of the ground and feel that he could get away from it all with just a flap of the wings. Summer camp with the Cadets was his first step toward his dream, and he felt, at this moment, watching planes with his mother and father, something beautiful was happening in his life.

"Closest things to angels," he declared.

That night, Jesse sat at his desk and worked on his religion project. It was due tomorrow, the eleventh of September.

It was his first major assignment, and he wanted to do well. Miss Simic told the class to pick the person they admired more than anybody else and put together a presentation that explained why they admired that person so much. Ryan said Jesse was crazy to be talking about his mother in front of the class. But Jesse felt as if he must. He admired her more than any other person, and the research was easy.

Jesse rummaged through his parents closet for a picture of his mother and after half an hour found the one that he was looking for. She was wearing a white dress and was standing so that the camera could see just how pregnant she really was. There was a smile on her face that told Jesse that she was happy to finally be carrying a baby to term.

Jesse turned the photo over and read the inscription on the back: *Me with my angel at eight months. Thanks to God!* Jesse walked back to his room and set himself to work.

The next morning, Jesse woke up with the feeling of being in a place he shouldn't have been. He was in the living room, having seen his parents off to work, but his mother hadn't called.

He looked at his watch. It was a quarter to eight. "Damn, I'm gonna be late for my presentation!" Jesse jumped off the couch, undressed on his way up the stairs, and almost jumped into the shower with his boxer shorts still on. He threw his uniform on in no particular order, and ran back downstairs to have a quick breakfast. He had no time to fix his hair or brush his teeth.

Jesse waited for his toast in the living room. He found the remote control between the pillows on the couch and turned on the television. A skyscraper was burning, and people were running for their lives. Jesse thought he had seen this film before. He turned off the television and left for school.

His knee was a little tender, but he walked as fast he could, reading over the cue cards and all the things he wanted to say. When he got to the end of his street Jesse almost tripped over his shoelace. He looked around and hoped that no one was around to see it. Jesse tied up his shoe, but when he stood up, he suddenly felt faint. He took a few steps and stopped again. Something wasn't right.

He felt uneasy and started to sweat. He looked up into an empty blue sky and was afraid. Instead of being moved by things he saw, he noticed nothing moving in the air. There wasn't a plane in sight.

Jesse gathered his wits and picked up the pace; he was late for his presentation and didn't want to let down his mother.

"...And so to sum up, I admire Britney Spears because by the time she was my age, she sold more than three million CDs and had people looking up to her, and I want people to look up to me, too." Sarah Vassals returned to her desk amidst half-hearted applause. Miss Simic thanked Sarah for her presentation and tallied up her mark.

"Jesse Cullen," she called out after a minute.

Jesse's heart jumped. It was his first high school presentation, and he wouldn't have Elly or Ryan there to wink or give him a thumbs-up. Daniel couldn't give a thumbs-up because he was too busy biting his nails, but he did look up at Jesse and smile.

Jesse was never good in front of an audience. Being made fun of at recess in front of thirty or forty people had a funny way of doing that to a boy. He heard a chuckle and hoped that it wasn't something he did. He stood at the front of the class and took a deep breath, waiting for Miss Simic's cue for him to begin.

"Okay, Jesse. Go ahead!"

He looked down at the picture of his mother holding him before he was even born. Jesse winked at her and hoped he did her proud. She deserved it.

Clearing his throat, Jesse looked at the first cue card and began his first high school presentation.

"The person I admire the most is—"

Suddenly, there was knock at the door. And then another, more urgent.

Miss Simic apologized to Jesse. "Just get settled and you can start over again when I get back."

Jesse watched her open the door and step out to the hall.

He looked at the picture of his mother and went over his introduction in his head one more time. Miss Simic walked back into the class—she was crying.

Suddenly, there was chaos in the halls. There were shouts of "Oh, my God," and "No fucking way," and the sound of feet running in the direction of the foyer.

Jesse figured it was just another fight. Two grade ten girls fought the other day in front of what must have been half the school. But when Jesse looked over at Miss Simic, he knew it was much worse. He felt a bead of sweat brew on his forehead, and his knee began to throb. He could hear Daniel biting his nails.

Over the PA system, Jesse heard his principal's voice: *"Ladies and Gentlemen, it is at this time that I ask you to bow your heads..."*

Jesse couldn't believe what he was seeing as he stared into the television.

"For those of you just joining us: At 8:46 this morning, American Airlines Flight eleven crashed into the World Trade Centre in New York. There are reports that the plane was hijacked, and it is highly unlikely that there are any survivors."

Jesse recognized the footage from this morning. It wasn't a film—it was real life. Someone shouted, "It's just like the movies!"

"What you are looking at is live footage of the World Trade Centre burning after being hit by a 747 earlier this morning."

Jesse was hypnotized, unable to take his eyes away from the images. On the screen, people were running for their lives, yelling, screaming, and looking for a place to hide.

Despite the fact that nearly half the school was in the library watching the footage of New York, the place was dead silent. But the silence crashed the moment a second plane crashed into the second tower.

Students screamed for their mothers and teacher's worried about their kids.

"Oh my god, oh my god, oh my god!"

"This is bad," Jesse whispered to himself as another teacher wept and a female student fainted just to the left of him.

"We have just received a report from a reliable source: it seems that the first plane was, indeed, hijacked and that it was a suicide mission. We have just got word from our Washington Bureau that Al-Qaeda, the terrorist group that blew up the American Embassy in Kenya, is claiming . . . " The newscaster couldn't finish her sentence. She was weeping. It was the first time Jesse had ever seen someone on the news cry after reporting a tragic story.

Breaking news was breaking every few seconds.

"Ladies and gentlemen, we have just received word that air space all over the United States has been closed and that all North American flights have been grounded. Any flights already on their way to the U.S. will be diverted to Canada. The FCC will be issuing a statement shortly."

Jesse turned around and felt the sudden urge to run. He exploded through the library doors, ran through the foyer, through the main entrance and directly outside, where he stood and looked up at an empty sky.

"Hey freak show, what are you looking for? Angels or something?"

"Fucking retard!"

Jesse ignored their taunts. He had more important things to worry about. He turned on the spot, hoping that there would be something in the sky—anything. The only thing that stood up to the vast emptiness was the crucifix atop the school.

Jesse's cell phone vibrated. It was a text message from Elly: *Call me.*

Jesse and Daniel spent the day in the chapel.

Rumours were circulating that the school was going to be closed for the day.

An announcement was made and all students were told to go back to their regularly scheduled class.

Most didn't.

When the bell rang to end what felt like the longest day in Jesse's history, the few remaining students in the chapel gathered their things and went to see their families.

Jesse walked home and, for the first time since he could remember, didn't once look up at the sky. "Closest thing to angels, my ass," he spit out and spat on the ground and walked inside his empty house and watched the news.

Immediatelty after dinner, Jesse turned on the television and flipped through the entire catalogue of channels: The History Channel, the Women's Network, the Comedy Network, the Men's Network, the Life Unscripted Channel, reality television.

Click.

Click.

Click.

The Discovery Channel, the Cooking Network, and the Sports Channel. He may have been changing the channels, but the stories and footage were of nothing but planes crashing into buildings and firemen and police officers escorting people to safety.

There were estimates that some twenty-five thousand people were believed dead and that there were thousands of causalities, including a thirteen-year-old boy who couldn't make sense of what he was seeing.

Jesse called Elly after supper. He was getting ready to leave to meet her at the park when his mother asked how he was doing.

"Not bad, Ma. I'm just thinking about all those people and their families. Twenty-five thousand the reporter said this afternoon."

He heard it in his head as many times as he had seen the plane crash on the news, on every channel at every hour.

"We have breaking news at this hour . . . "

" . . . twenty-five thousand . . . "

Jesse couldn't make sense of the number. Twenty-five thousand. But the size didn't matter—one casualty was more than enough.

"Honey, are you sure you're okay?"

Jesse thought about the number of times in his life he had heard her ask that same question; too many times for a mother of a thirteen-year-old child.

It was the first time Jesse and Elly had seen each other since school started.

They greeted one another with a longer than normal hug and walked over to a bench, sitting under the same tree they used to climb in the summertime. They sat silently for a moment, watching the neighbourhood kids play cops and robbers and hide-and-seek.

Jesse couldn't keep his eyes off a young boy making paper airplanes. He watched the kid toss the plane, which sailed all of three feet before crashing to the ground in front of him. Disappointed, the boy picked up the paper plane and tore it into pieces.

"This sucks! All they do is crash."

"Where were you when it happened?" Elly asked, pronouncing the word 'it' as if *it* would always be i*t*.

He told her that he was sleeping on the couch when it happened. "Why do you ask?"

"It's one of those days where everybody will know where they were when it happened. I was in the washroom. A bunch of girls came in screaming. One girl wondered if any celebrities had been killed and started to bawl."

Jesse's mind was like a slide-show, one image to the next: one plane, one tower, two planes, two towers, twenty-five thousand dead including firemen, policemen, janitors, mothers, fathers, siblings, friends, and children.

He was shaking.

"What's wrong?" Elly asked as she put her arm around him, hoping to settle him down.

Because she was Elly and because she was the most beautiful best-friend in the world, he stood up, wiped his tears, and told her.

"Did you hear what the president was reading when he found out about the attacks?"

"No."

"He was reading *My Pet Goat* to a bunch of third graders in Florida. That was my favourite book. Well, it was until Rudy Sinclair took it from me one day. He said that because I had ADHD, I couldn't read it. So he just up and fucking took it—the same book the president was reading when he found out about the attacks!"

"What's your point, babe?"

Jesse sighed and was a quiet for a seconds before he answered. "There is no point. I'm just talkin' shit."

"Tell me," Elly pleaded.

"Seeing those planes crash into that building really messed me up, Elly."

Elly had always counted planes with him and had gone to the airport with him to watch them land. She understood what they meant to him.

"I know it did, Jesse."

"No, listen: I'm telling you—it really messed me up. When the first plane hit, I knew I was wounded for life, but when that second one hit, I knew something had died in me forever and—," he paused.

"Go on," she whispered.

"I don't want to fly planes anymore."

Jesse exhaled as if to rid his body of any further thought of being a pilot.

"Jess, you can't go on talking like that. If you change your life because of what terrorists do, then they've won."

"Well, I've changed enough of my life for those fucking terrorists at school. Why should this be any different?"

"Terrorists at school? What are you talking about, Jesse?"

"That's what those guys in school are: terrorists. Only, their weapons are words, and sometimes rocks or bottles. I was watching the news after school today, and seeing the images of all those people running away reminded me of running through the hallway so that I could call my mom to come get me. I know that's selfish of me, but I couldn't stop thinking about it."

She put her arm around him and turned his face so that she could look him in the eye. "You know what these tragedies are good for, Jesse?"

"No."

"Bringing people together."

"Yeah, but it shouldn't take a tragedy for that to happen."

When he got home, Jesse joined his parents. His father was watching the news, his mother reading the paper. Posted on every channel were faces of the terrorists with names that Jesse couldn't pronounce, but tried to under his breath.

He couldn't believe what he was seeing, especially the footage of people standing out on the ledge of the building, too far up to jump and land safely. But they jumped nonetheless, because they couldn't stand the thought of burning to death.

It was one thing to see a tall building crumble, but it was another thing entirely to see people falling from that high up.

Jesse looked over at his mom. "Mom, do people who kill themselves go to heaven?"

"No, honey, they don't."

"Does that mean that those people who jumped today won't go to heaven?

She put down the newspaper and cleared her throat.

"I think I remember reading once that it depended on the circumstances that drove the person to kill themselves. And if that's the case, I'm sure those poor souls are resting with God now."

Jesse had seen enough. He kissed his mother on the cheek and patted his father on the shoulder. "I love you, guys. Good night."

He changed into his pyjamas as if on remote control.

Twenty-five thousand people were reported dead, and the weapon that killed them hung, toy-sized, above his bed in the same spot it had been since his first day of school. He walked over to his desk and found the scissors and cut the string that held the plane that Jesse no longer wanted to fly.

"Fuck toys," he cursed, and walked to his open window.

He stood there, staring, for a few seconds and felt as if the sky was mocking him. He lifted the toy plane as if it were made of paper and tossed it out the window, watching it crash in his neighbour's backyard. He prayed for the souls of all those people who had no choice but to take their own lives and looked down at the damage that he had just caused.

"At least I didn't hurt anyone."

Jesse thought of the little boy at the park earlier in the evening.

All they do is crash!

He shut his window and cried himself to sleep.

CHAPTER TEN

It was a time of unprecedented global solidarity. Countries from around the world extended their condolences and offered their military support to avenge the attacks on New York City and the United States of America. World leaders encouraged their constituents to be vigilant and show no signs of fear. Citizens wanted revenge and, judging by the reports on the news, revenge was coming- soon.

There was talk of war on the news programs, all the talk shows, and even the Weather Network. Experts were predicting that the war would be an unconventional one and that it could go on for a very long time. The war hadn't even begun, yet Jesse was already feeling like a casualty.

He sat on the couch and waited anxiously for the president of the United States of America to appear on the screen. He was set to address the nation at nine a.m., and when Jesse saw him walk up to the lectern, he reached for the remote and turned up the volume.

"On my orders, the United States military has begun strikes against Al-Qaeda terrorist training camps and military installations of the Taliban regime in Afghanistan."

Jesse could barely remember the Gulf War and never thought he'd get a chance to see another one. Jesse's understanding of war would no longer be based on video games, books, and an old man's recollection—this was going to be the real thing.

Jesse listened intently.

"*... An attack on one is an attack on all... This will be an age of liberty... Every grief recedes with time and grace...*"

Jesse wondered when his own personal grief was going to gracefully recede. He no longer wanted to fly planes, war was being declared, and his leg was in a cast.

After the president had blessed the American people, Jesse pushed himself up off the couch. His mother jumped from her seat and picked up Jesse's crutches.

"It's okay, Mom. I can do it on my own." He took the crutches from his mother and set them under his arms. Jesse struggled up the stairs and imagined himself a casualty of an unconventional war with no end in sight. He wished he didn't have to go to school tomorrow.

Jesse's mother drove him to school the next day. She dropped him off at the side entrance. Jesse at least wanted to make it inside the school before anyone on the outside had a chance to make fun of him.

"If you need anything, honey, call me at work!" She blew Jesse a kiss and didn't drive away until her little, wounded soldier was safely inside the school.

Mr. Simmons, Jesse's vice-principal, was waiting for him at the elevator. He smiled when he saw Jesse and began rifling through his pocket.

He pulled out the elevator key and handed it to Jesse, first showing him how to use it. Mr. Simmons wished Jesse good luck and walked back into the main office. Jesse limped into and out of the elevator and hobbled to the chapel. He told Daniel he would meet him there before class.

Morning prayer was about to begin. Jesse took the last available seat. He looked over at Miss Simic, smiled, and waved.

Jesse liked her. The smile on her face told most of the class that she loved what she was doing and that she was happy to be doing it, though some in the class took advantage of her caring nature. Last week, after Miss Simic told him to go to the office for a uniform violation, Giancarlo Rossi had picked up the overhead projector and threw it against the blackboard where it smashed liked a bomb and crashed to the floor. Most students had sat there in shock, including Jesse, but a few laughed because they thought it was just that funny. Miss Simic dismissed the class a few minutes before the bell and didn't show up for work the next day.

Since September eleventh, violence was all the rage. The tension that gripped the global community had filtered into the hallways and classrooms of St. Elizabeth's.

President Bush declared war on some country far away in the Middle East, and the whole world was sent into turmoil— St. Elizabeth's was another soldier's playground.

Shock and awe, the military strategy championed by the government, made its way into the hallways, and the casualties were mounting. Punches were thrown, noses broken, teeth cracked, eyes bruised.

Ryan was suspended for pulling a knife when someone tried to hustle some money from him on his way out of the cafeteria. There were reports of extortion, gambling, and there was even a rumour that a few of the grade nine girls were selling blow jobs in the washroom.

Morning prayer and the national anthem now followed by stern warnings from the principal. He encouraged people to follow the footsteps of Christ.

Jesse liked the idea—he just wished he didn't have to do it with his leg in a cast. It wasn't a good time to be in the halls.

Jesse recalled hearing on the news that the attacks would force people to reassess their lives, to change their values and consider what was really important. There were reports that church attendance was on the rise and that the world was experiencing a spiritual rebirth. It didn't look that way to Jesse. The chapel was empty and, because of that, he spent more time in it

On his way outside to meet Daniel for lunch, Jesse overheard a couple of girls talking about Jennifer Lopez's wedding.

"I wonder what her dress looked like!"

"She must have looked so hot!"

Jesse couldn't understand how something as trivial as a celebrity wedding could matter to people when a war was going on and people were being killed. He walked away in disbelief and met Daniel outside for lunch.

They sat in their favourite spot, only this time Jesse sat on the rock because he couldn't bend his leg. They traded bananas for oranges and a pop for chocolate milk.

Daniel was quiet. Jesse talked about the war.

"You know, Daniel, sometimes it feels like the whole world is at war!"

Jesse waited for Daniel to say something. He looked over at him and could see that he wasn't paying attention.

He was watching two male students pushing around Salisha Mohammed, a girl from their religion class. They were pointing and jeering.

"Hey, was that your uncle that hijacked that plane?"

"No, wait, I bet it was your dad!"

"Are you a terrorist?"

"I hope you're a suicide bomber. Just don't hurt anyone but yourself!"

Jesse listened to the words that were shot out of their mouths like bullets.

"Why don't you take that stupid scarf off your face?"

Their jabbing turned to pushing, and Salisha dropped her books.

A sudden swirl of guilt consumed Jesse's body. He needed to help her in the way he should have helped Derwin, the way all those people who ever stood around and watched Jesse get picked on should have helped him.

"Shouldn't we do something?" he asked Daniel, hoping he'd have a plan because Jesse was having a difficult time coming up with one on his own.

Daniel looked at Jesse's leg and continued biting his nails, knowing Jesse wouldn't be much help. They watched Salisha run away, another casualty of war.

Daniel set down his sandwich and walked across the parking lot, over the sidewalk, and across the street.

He picked up Salisha's Bible and walked back to Jesse.

Jesse looked at his watch and asked Daniel to help him with his crutches.

"I'm going to the chapel. I want to speak to Ms. Harper."

Ms. Harper was on the phone in her office. Daniel took a seat, but Jesse didn't feel like sitting—it was too much work for someone with a bum knee—so he limped around the chapel and tried to take his mind off things.

He stopped at the statue of Jesus.

Jesus was taller than Jesse. His hands were held up to his side, the palms facing outward. Jesse looked at the holes that the nails had made and tried to imagine what it must have felt like to be crucified. He looked at the face of Jesus and felt like he had a pretty good idea.

He knew enough about Jesus to know that He was condemned to death, that a friend had betrayed Him, and that He rose on the third day. Jesse took his eyes off of the statue and looked over at the Stations of the Cross that lined the wall to Jesse's right. He turned his back on Jesus and hobbled over to the first station: Jesus is condemned to die.

Jesse limped along with Jesus on His way to being crucified, and stopped at the twelfth station. He looked at Jesus, dead on the cross. He looked at the scars on his body, the thorns on his head, and the sign that he could never remember the translation of.

Jesse stared at Jesus nailed to the cross, His feet off the ground, His arms outstretched like a bird—like a plane—and Jesse felt something very strange. He couldn't make sense of it, but Jesse was feeling an affinity to the man that was nailed to the cross for the sins of humanity. "You died for our sins, and this is how we pay you back," Jesse muttered apologetically.

"Sorry, Jesse."

Jesse was startled. Where had the voice come from?

He didn't see Ms. Harper standing beside him.

She motioned for Jesse to sit down.

Ms. Harper looked down at Jesse's leg. "What happened?"

"Growing pains," Jesse answered. "Ms. Harper, I have a stupid question to ask you."

"Jesse there is no such thing as a stupid question. The only stupid questions are the ones that are never asked."

Jesse's question stopped being stupid when he finally asked it: "Are bullies terrorists?"

"That's a good question, Jesse. Appropriate, to say the least!" She was silent for a few seconds, then put her hand on Jesse's knee. "Bullies *are* like terrorists. What they inflict is emotional terrorism, terrorizing an individual or small group of individuals for their own good. They may not use guns or bombs or grenades or planes, but they have the most powerful weapon of all. They use words, which are more destructive than all of those things put together. Words are the real weapons of mass destruction, Jesse."

Jesse recalled the day he had told Elly that exact same thing.

Before he could get up, Ms. Harper rifled through her pockets, pulled out a pen, and asked Daniel for a piece of paper. "Here, Jesse. I want you to read this passage in the Bible, and then come back and tell me what you think."

It had been a long day, and Jesse was tired. He opened his locker and packed his bag. Jesse worked his way through the halls, squeezing past the hordes of students who always took too long to say goodbye. He headed for the exit, but saw Martin and Rudy walking back into the school.

Jesse's immediate inclination was turn and go in the other direction, but he only had one good leg and his mother was waiting for him. He took a deep breath and proceeded through the doors.

"Yo! Get a load of gimp-boy," they mocked.

"Whatever is wrong with your leg, it can't be as bad as your face!"

They made fun of his acne and asked him if he still liked to masturbate.

"Are you blind yet?"

Jesse feared that one of them would take his crutch from him and push him down to the ground. He was almost through the door when Martin hollered, "If you think you can hide from me and my boy, you are sorely mistaken."

Jesse walked through the doors and was happy to be out of the building.

Before he got to the van, Jesse stopped. Something familiar struck him. He had heard what Martin said somewhere else and tried to figure it out. Then he remembered: Last night, President Bush uttered a similar threat when a reporter asked him about the hunt for Osama bin Laden. *"If he thinks he can hide from us and our allies, he his sorely mistaken."*

121

"Fucking war," Jesse griped. He wished that someone would hunt down Martin Paynesworth and Rudy Sinclair.

Jesse had thought about war and violence enough throughout the day, so he didn't watch television with his parents that night. After supper, he went straight to his room to get a head start on his homework. He took his books out from his school bag andsat with Sali sha's Bible in his hands. He opened it up to the flyleaf, where all the names of the students that read it were inscribed. The third name, Jason Thompson, caught Jesse's attention.

Jason's younger sister, Samantha, had been Jesse's classmate in grade three. She went home one day after school and found her brother hanging from a tree, with a rope around his neck and blood dripping from his mouth.

Jesse remembered that day as if it were yesterday.

People were shocked because Jason was one of the more popular students at St. Elizabeth's. He was captain of the football team and was a favourite with all the girls.

Jesse tried to remember what Samantha looked like, but couldn't. He knew what Jason Thompson looked like though, because his picture hung in the Hall of Heroes.

Jesse couldn't figure out why someone who had killed himself had his picture hanging alongside pictures of graduating classes, former principals, the names of honour roll students, and trophies from school championships.

Jesse turned the pages of the Bible until he found the passage that Ms. Harper had suggested he read. Every word was highlighted; every sentence was underlined. It looked to Jesse like someone else had gotten the point of it before he had a chance to. He wondered if it was Jason Thompson or Salisha, then he read the passage:

Those who pay heed to slander,
will not find rest

Nor will they settle down in peace.
The blow of a whip raises a
welt, but a blow of the tongue
crushes the bones.
Many have fallen by the edge of
the sword,
But not as many have fallen
Because of the tongue.
Happy is the one who is
Protected from it,
Who has not been exposed to
Its anger
Who has not been borne its yoke,
and has not been bound by its
shackles.
For its yoke is a yoke of iron,
And its fetters are fetters of
bronze.
Its death is an evil death,
And Hell is preferable to it.

Jesse didn't need to underline it to prove to himself that he got the point of the passage. He sat up in his chair and ran his fingers through his hair.

"Now this is what we should be reading in school!"

But instead of feeling like he had found the answer to a problem that he longed to solve, Jesse was sad and felt all the more hopeless. The Bible was written over two thousand years ago. It was studied in schools, read aloud on Sundays, and was supposed to represent the word of God.

He thought about Vanessa Musgrove and the eraser, Samantha and her dead brother, Derwin and his taped mouth, Daniel and his nails, Salisha and her Bible, and Jason Thompson and his smile.

He was suddenly very conscious of the acne on his face, and his knee began to throb.

He thought about all the things that Mr. George fought for, all of the children who lost parents on September eleventh, and all the children that didn't get to hear the ending of *My Pet Goat*. He remembered how he used to want to fly a plane.

The world seemed like such a sad place. Planes were used as weapons and bullies took words straight from the president's mouth.

In religion class the next day, Jesse hoped that Salisha would show up so that he could give her back her Bible. But she didn't show up for class that day, and something told Jesse that she wouldn't be coming the next day either.

Another victim.

He was beginning to feel hopeless, helpless, useless, and just less human. It seemed like the older he got, the more anxious he became. He would rather be thinking about things like girls and games and just being a kid. But local events and global wars kept him from doing that. He couldn't think like a kid because he wasn't allowed to be one. He wasn't an adult, but he was expected to act like one: to fend for himself, to start a war, to be on the offensive, and to watch the casualties mount.

Jesse was tired. It was only first period.

He thought about the Sirrach passage and couldn't agree more: *"Its death is an evil death, and Hell is preferable to it!"*

CHAPTER ELEVEN

The war in Afghanistan was over. The Coalition forces had successfully chased the Taliban regime out of Afghanistan, but Osama bin Laden was still on the loose; Jesse's cast was off, Martin and Rudy still patrolled the hall, and Salisha Mohammed was nowhere to be found.

Jesse never admitted it to anyone, but he was a little sad to see the cast go. It may have slowed him down, but he liked the fringe benefits that came with being a wounded kid. His parents paid even more attention to him, and so did some of the older girls at school. They signed his cast and made him blush.

He also liked having the distinction of being the only student who was allowed to use the elevator. He had promised the vice-principal that he wouldn't bring anyone on with him, but Jesse knew that Daniel wanted to be out of the halls just as much as he did and so took him along for the ride sometimes. They were allowed to enjoy so little of high school and what it had to offer, so Jesse and Daniel rode the elevator like it was a ride at an amusement park. Daniel never once chewed his nails on the way up.

Daniel told Jesse that he had started biting his fingernails around the same time he was old enough to figure out the difference between talking loudly and fighting—the latter being something his parents did far too much of before they split up and tried to forget about one another.

"When I saw my father hit my mom, I knew I couldn't do anything about it, so I just bit my nails. I think it was because I needed something to spit. The worst part was that at night I would lie in my bed and listen to my mother cry from her room, and when I'd wake up, some mornings my fingers would be bleeding. She bought me the rosary so that it would keep my hands busy and out of my mouth. It worked until I started high school. I came from a town of six hundred and fifty people, and now I'm in a school that has a population three times that size. What else am I supposed to do but bite my nails?"

.Yesterday was their last ride in the elevator. Jesse was getting his cast off, and he had to return the key. On the way down to the first floor, Daniel looked over at Jesse and thanked him.

"For what?"

Daniel looked around the elevator. "For letting me take this with you. I like it. It's in-between floors; neither here nor there. It's neat. What do you like about it?"

Jesse shrugged his shoulders. "I don't know, man. If I have to like just one thing about it, I'd have to say it's getting my feet off the ground. Its almost like flying, I guess."

They walked out of the elevator and returned the key.

The student body was too caught up in plans for the upcoming Halloween dance to worry about bombs, bullets, bullies, or casualties.

The halls were filled with anxious voices as students yelled their plans, text-messaged their dates, and set out to find the coolest costume. They talked about the dance like it was graduation all over again.

Jesse remembered when Halloween was about tricks and treats, when it didn't matter if your Ninja Turtle mask was held together with tape. It was about being a kid. Now it was about looking good, which felt just like stepping out of one costume and into another, making sure that everything was in its place because you never knew who might be watching.

Things only got worse when the Student Council announced that students didn't have to wear their uniforms to school on the day of the dance. There was a roar throughout the cafeteria that spilled out to the halls and seeped into every classroom.

Jesse had gone to a couple of dances in elementary school, but when his acne got bad and the jokes even worse, he avoided them altogether.

He hadn't even considered the possibility of going to the dance until Daniel said it might be a good idea if they went.

Jesse looked at him and laughed. "Why?"

"I don't know. It might be fun to see everyone dressed up in their costumes."

"You don't have to go to a Halloween dance to see that, Daniel!"

Daniel stood up and spoke with an enthusiasm that surprised Jesse. "I already figured it out, Jesse: we'll wear masks! You don't have to worry about anything when you wear a mask."

It was perverted logic, but Jesse conceded that he had a point. It was a chance to try and be someone else, since everybody else was doing it.

They were excited because for once they were going to feel like a part of the school community. Up till now, that community consisted of a classroom, a chapel, and a corner outside where they ate their lunch. They agreed that they had to make a statement and that their costumes had to get people's attentions, something they tried to avoid every other day of the year.

Daniel screamed as he tried to pull away from Elly.

"Hold still, damn it!" Elly grabbed a pin from her mouth and pulled the fabric tighter beneath Daniel's armpit. When she was done, she tightened the rope around Daniel's waist, and helped Jesse with his tie.

"There—I think we're pretty much done!"

Elly looked at the two of them. "Okay. So, Daniel's a shepherd, and you're a stockbroker? I thought you said I'd be impressed with the concept? I don't get it."

Jesse wanted to keep their costumes a surprise for as long as they could. He walked out of the room for a minute and came back holding a mask in each hand. He passed Daniel his mask, and they turned their backs to Elly.

"What the—"

The boys turned around at the same time.

"Well, what do you think?" Jesse asked eagerly.

"Oh, man. You guys look awesome! Osama bin Laden and George W. Bush. I love it!" She skipped over to the adversaries and gave them a hug.

Jesse blushed from behind his mask. "Not bad, eh?"

Elly could barely contain herself. "Hold on!"

She ran to her purse and came back with her camera-phone. "Stand side by side, and put your arms around one another!"

Osama and George obeyed.

"Perfect! Now that's what the world needs: a little friendship."

They couldn't agree more.

"Say cheese!"

"Hey, what is it about cheese that makes for good pictures?" Jesse asked for the second time in his life.

Daniel chuckled, "How do you say cheese in Saudi?"

Elly picked up her bag and wished the two of them luck.

"You sure you can't come tomorrow, Elly? You don't need a costume. Just come as you are," Jesse pleaded.

"No, Jesse! I have to work on my project for Monday. And besides, every day is Halloween at my school. There may not be any candy or treats, but there are a lot of costumes, and there are certainly plenty of monsters. You two have a great time tomorrow night!"

The school was a much brighter place the next day. Instead of grey pants and blue sweaters, the halls were brightened with colours and flesh tones. It was a fashion gala, everyone going to extremes with bright colours, white shoes, fresh tans, heels, fancy hats, belly buttons, g-strings, short skirts, tight shirts, more hats, and blue bandanas. It was a coming-out party. From the gel in their hair to the sparkle of their newly bleached set of teeth, everything glistened. The hallways were the catwalks, and everyone wanted to be a model.

But to Jesse (dressed in his Colorado jersey, jeans, white sneakers, and yellow hat) it looked like everyone was still in full uniform. They may have been wearing basketball jerseys with different team names and colours, but they were still wearing basketball jerseys or mini-skirts—uniforms determined by what they saw in music videos and magazines.

At lunch, Jesse and Daniel ate their sandwiches and talked about the dance and their costumes and tried to figure out what people might think about them. Jesse watched the students from the special-education class walk around the parking lot picking up garbage and recognized one of the boys at the front of the group. He was the boy that emptied the recycle bins for Ms. Simic's class. He always waved to the class before he shut the door.

Daniel put down his sandwich and smiled. "You know what's funny? I heard someone the other day make fun of some of those kids because they smile all the time. Can you imagine making fun of someone because they smile a lot?"

They were in the middle of another game of Go Fish when Jesse noticed a shadow on the wall behind Daniel.

It unnerved Jesse to know that someone was standing behind him, but when he saw the shadow wave, he had a pretty good idea who it was. Jesse invited him to sit down and held up the cards as an invitation to play. Jesse moved over and dealt a hand to their new friend.

From what they understood, his name was Mike, and they let him believe that he had won every hand until it was time go. Class was beginning in ten minutes, so Jesse tried to figure out a polite way to interrupt Mike, who was telling another story. Jesse and Daniel stood up. Jesse was about to invite Mike for another game tomorrow, but he was interrupted.

"Well, well, well. What do we have here?"

Jesse recognized the voice and was afraid. He looked over at Daniel who was suddenly looking very tense.

It was Billy, the guy that wore his football jacket like a trophy and knew how to work a crowd. Only this time, there were five guys wearing football jackets. It may have been dress-down day, but it wasn't difficult to see that they were part of the same team and that Billy was the captain.

"Hey, look at all the retards."

His teammates cheered him on.

Mike took their laughter as a gesture of goodwill and waved incessantly.

Daniel started biting his nails.

They were pinned against the wall and facing an offensive line. Jesse could see no way for them to defend themselves.

Billy thrust his finger into Daniel's chest.

"I thought I told you to stay out of my way!"

"I . . . I . . ." Daniel was trembling.

Jesse looked round for help but could barely see over the wall of shoulders. He was too afraid to stand on his toes, since any sudden movement might set the team off.

Just then, the doors outside the cafeteria opened, and Jesse prayed that it was a teacher. When he saw who it was, he thought his prayers were answered in more ways than one.

It was Mr. Ridley, a religion teacher, and he was dressed up as Moses. He was a wearing a white robe, and his hair hung past his shoulders. He was carrying a staff in his right hand and was pointing at something with his left. From what Jesse could tell, he was reciting the Ten Commandments.

Jesse tried to muster up the courage to scream for help, but when he tried, no sound came out of his mouth.

Billy looked at all three of them and cursed, "God, you guys are fucking losers!"

Moses yelled: "You shall not take the name of the Lord your God in vain."

Billy scowled: "When are you gonna get rid of that acne, motherfucker?"

Moses warned: "Honour your father and your mother."

Billy confessed: "I heard that you're gay."

Moses declared: "You shall not bear false witness against your neighbour."

When Moses was finished, he banged his staff on the pavement. When Billy was finished, he banged his right fist into his left palm.

Jesse stared at Moses, posing for pictures with students that didn't really need his help.

"Excuse me, is there a problem here?"

Everyone was startled by the adult voice. It was the special-ed teacher.

Billy and his friends took a step back, but didn't take their eyes off of their prey.

"Mike, its time for you to come back to class. Come on!"

Mike smiled at the group and waved goodbye.

The teacher stood at the door and waited for the crowd to disperse.

Billy pointed at Daniel and warned him, "You better not show up at the dance tonight!"

Jesse and Daniel stood in silence, watching Mike turn and wave again before he walked into the school.

Moses was finished for the day. He held the door open for the bullies, nodding hello as they passed. He turned to go inside the school, but turned around one last time to shout, "Remember what I have told you here today. Don't be afraid, God is testing you!"

"Some test," Jesse muttered.

After lunch, Jesse failed his science quiz because he couldn't stop thinking about Moses, who had been too busy preaching to help.

Ryan showed up to computer class for the first time that week, and was dressed in full hip-hop gear: a Boston Celtics' jersey, a 76'ers hat, Vince Carter sneakers, and a chain that was supposed to look more expensive than it actually was.

"Yo, where you been, man? I've been calling you . . ."

He was lying.

" . . . but I didn't bother leaving a message."

Jesse smirked.

"Listen, man, do you think I can borrow your computer notes? I'm pretty much screwed for midterms, and you know how my dad feels about failing."

Jesse remembered the French test that kept Ryan from going to cadets, and, because it was Ryan that was changing, not him, Jesse handed over his binder.

Ryan took the binder and stuffed it into his bag. "You going to the dance tonight?"

"I was going to, but I don't think I'm going anymore." Jesse told him what happened at lunch, but didn't bother with the Moses bit. He figured Ryan wouldn't understand.

Ryan looked at Jesse and shook his head. "You know what happened when I got suspended for having that knife in my hand? They told me I had to take an anger management course—me! Like I'm the one with the problem, man. You've got to understand, Jesse, that no one is going to help you with your problems; you've got to take care of them yourself."

Ryan's face became very serious before he continued, "You can't let people stop you from doing things. None of those damn guys have said anything to me since I was suspended—not even Martin or Rudy. When those cops walked me out of the school in handcuffs, they did me the biggest favour ever."

Mr. Darpinder asked Ryan to be quiet. When he turned back to face the whiteboard, Ryan carried on.

"Who's that guy I see you with all the time?"

"A friend."

"Why does he bite his nails so much?

"Habit, I guess."

"Some habit, man." Ryan bit his nail and spit it on the floor.

Mr. Darpinder stopped teaching, marched to the back of class, and towered over Ryan, who looked up at the teacher and smirked.

"I thought I told you to stop talking. I want you to pack up your things and go to the office. The least you can do when you show up to class is pay attention."

Ryan threw back his chair and cursed under his breath.

"I gotta run, man. Thanks for the notes. Hope to see ya at the dance tonight."

Jesse watched Ryan limp out of class and strut his way into the halls.

Daniel showed up at six with his costume. When they were finally dressed, they looked at one another and shook hands for world peace.

"The most powerful man in the world!" Jesse proclaimed.

"The most feared man in the world!" Daniel exclaimed.

They both secretly wished that Halloween could go on forever. There was an awkward silence until Daniel broke it.

"I'm a little nervous."

"Me, too. Today scared the shit out of me," Jesse admitted from beneath his mask.

"I know. But we can't expect not to enjoy ourselves, right? Besides, we'll be wearing masks and we can finally be ourselves."

Jesse liked the sound of that. "Let's go!"

Jack-o'-lanterns burned, and children ran from house to house hoping more for a treat than a trick. Jesse and Daniel walked back to St. Elizabeth's, waving at all the cars that honked and the people that encouraged them.

"Yeah, right on man!"

"That's what we need, baby!"

"I wish."

Someone shouted, "Thank you."

Jesse smiled.

It may have been 8:00 at night, but the scene in front of the school made it feel like eight o'clock in the morning. The bus shelter was overflowing with students, and cars rolled by at a snail's pace.

Jesse and Daniel worked their way through the crowd, but instead of being harassed like every other day, they accepted compliments and laughed. Jesse smelled pot and thought he heard Ryan's voice. He turned around but couldn't make out who was who—he was facing six guys dressed as soldiers. They wore fatigues and their faces were camouflaged.

Daniel joked, "If you're the Commander in Chief, you should send those guys to some far-off war!"

"If only it were that easy," Jesse responded. "If only."

The foyer had been transformed into a haunted house. Toilet paper hung from the walls, and ghosts made out of garbage bags hung from the lower parts of the ceiling. The crucifix that stood in the middle of the foyer was covered in cobwebs.

While walking through the Hall of Heroes, Jesse snuck at peek at Jason Thompson's picture. In the background, ghosts were howling and women were screaming.

Jesse's spine tingled.

There was a lineup to get into the gym. Teachers were checking student ID cards, so the line moved slowly. Jesse checked out all the costumes as he waited.

There were five or six cowboys and a couple of Indians. Some of the girls were dressed up as Barbie dolls, others as their favourite singers: Beyoncé, Missy Elliot, Madonna, Britney, Christina, Gwen. Amongst the boys, rappers and gangsters were the costumes of choice: Jay-Z, Snoop Dogg, Ludacris, Nelly—all sorts of gangsters, pimps, wanksters, and pranksters.

Jesse spotted the American soldiers. One of them saluted Jesse, and another pointed at Daniel.

When they were finally at the front of the line, Jesse passed his student card to Miss Simic. She was inside a cardboard box that was being held up by a string tied around the back of her neck. The front of the box was decorated with a pot and a frying pan with two eggs painted on the inside of it.

She was the prettiest stove that Jesse had ever seen.

She looked down at Jesse's card. When she realized who it was behind the mask, she looked at him and laughed. "You look great, Jesse!"

Jesse wished she hadn't said his name so loud.

She handed Daniel back his card and complimented them both.

"Two boys doing more for world peace than most adults! I love it!"

The gym floor was littered with bodies. Chaperons walked through the dance floor, while the police tried to remain visible. At first, Jesse thought they were students in costume, but looking closer he could see that those were real bulletproof vests and guns.

Jesse was starting to feel warm. He was sweating behind his mask.

"Hey, Daniel, do you want a dri—," Jesse didn't finish his question because Daniel was no longer standing beside him.

He was on the dance floor.

Jesse laughed. The whole world was looking for Osama bin Laden, and there he was, out on the dance floor getting down to Destiny's Child.

Jesse walked over to the refreshment stand and asked for a pop.

"Excuse me, Mr. Bush!"

Jesse forgot who he was for a second, but when he realized the voice was directed at him, he turned around to see a girl with a bone in her hair looking right at him. She was wearing a leopard print dress, and Jesse couldn't take his eyes off of her cleavage.

She smiled.

"I'm Wilma Flintstone! I'm assuming you're George Bush. I love your costume!"

Jesse shook her hand. "My name's Jes—uh, George Bush. Nice to meet you!"

He opened his drink and was about to take a sip, when he realized he couldn't because he was wearing a mask. Jesse turned around asked for a straw.

Wilma asked for two diet pops and looked over at Jesse.

"Do you wanna dance later?"

Jesse's heart was racing. "Sure!"

Wilma grabbed her drinks and went back out on to the dance floor. She handed Britney Spears her pop and pointed her in Jesse's direction. They both waved. Jesse waved back. He wished he could always wear a mask.

The dance floor was crowded and Jesse had a difficult time finding Daniel.

When he finally spotted him, he watched him dancing with a group of Barbie dolls and divas. A group began to gather around them and form a circle.

Daniel had an audience, and Jesse wished he could have the same. In a small way, he envied Daniel. He was a small kid, nervous, but wasn't afraid to try new things. He was out on the dance floor holding court. People were laughing with him, not at him.

Jesse was watching his schoolmates dance away the night, when he spotted the American soldiers working their way through the dance floor. He could see that they were upset that the crowd had gone from watching them dance, to watching Osama bin Laden. They leaned into one another and whispered something back and forth into each other's ear. They were offended and wanted revenge.

The regiment worked their way through the crowd like sharks in shallow water. Jesse watched them surround Daniel. They started dancing, holding their rifles above their heads with both hands, and marching to a uniform beat.

One of them poked at Daniel with his rifle. Daniel tried to move away, but they formed a tighter circle.

Daniel stopped dancing. He looked vulnerable, like the day in the cafeteria when he reminded Jesse of a three-legged zebra. Daniel tried to walk through the battalion, but they wouldn't let him pass.

Jesse dropped his pop and rushed out to the dance floor.

There was a lot of pushing and fighting. A cowboy looked at an Indian and punched him in the head. Chaos erupted as Jesse clawed his way through the crowd to try and help Daniel. Some thought it was choreographed dance and were whistling and clapping along. The police thought otherwise.

The lights were turned on, and the police in the middle of the melee told everyone to get out of the gym. They looked nervous—there were a lot of plastic guns, and they were afraid that one of them might be real. They gym was evacuated and students were told to leave.

Jesse asked a police officer if he could stay with Daniel, who the police were now questioning.

"I think it'll be better if you wait outside, son."

On his way out the door, Jesse stepped on the can of pop that he had dropped. It was empty, and the pop drowned Jesse's sole in what looked like blood.

Outside, Jesse kept an eye out for Daniel from across the street. There were still a lot of students hanging out in front of the school, and Jesse didn't want to take any chances. He was leaning up against a tree when he saw Wilma and Britney Spears walking towards him. Jesse took a deep breath. He was hoping that something good might come from the night. He stepped in front of the two girls. "Hey!"

"Can I help you?" Wilma asked, looking as if she had never asked Jesse to dance.

"Yeah! We met inside. George Bush, remember?" Jesse pointed to his mask.

"No, I don't think so. I would certainly remember a face like that," she spit back and turned around, pretending that Jesse wasn't there.

Jesse felt a hand on his shoulder. It was Daniel, holding Jesse's mask in his hand.

The crowd outside began to disperse. Jesse thought it was a good idea to head home. While they waited for the light to turn green, another light caught Jesse's eye. He looked into the bus shelter where a Barbie doll was passing something to a soldier.

It was the soldier that Jesse recognized out on the dance floor. His camouflage make-up was reduced to a smudge across his cheek. Jesse watched him take a haul from a joint and send a cloud of smoke cascading onto the sidewalk. Jesse recognized his eyes. It was Ryan.

"It was fun for a while, wasn't it?" Daniel asked trying to maintain his composure.

"I guess," Jesse responded. He couldn't take his eyes off Ryan.

"For a second there, I actually felt like I belonged."

"Yeah. Me, too."

Jesse almost jumped out of his skin when a car honked and someone hollered, "Nice try losers!"

A muffler roared. "Keep dreaming."

Somebody laughed, "You fucking wish!"

Daniel suddenly jumped ahead of Jesse and, with his fist in the air, screamed, "At least we tried, you stupid mother-fuckers!" When Daniel saw the car slow down, he lowered his head and whispered, "At least we tried."

The car burned rubber and ran a yellow light. A police car that was pulling out of the school parking lot flashed its sirens and took off in pursuit.

Jesse found the nearest trash bin and ditched his mask.

"Looks like this war is never going to end."

CHAPTER TWELVE

The streets mirrored the battlefields Jesse had seen on television over the past couple of months. Jack-o'-lanterns were smashed to bits, missing more than a few teeth. Toilet paper hung lifelessly from the bare branches of dead trees, and garbage lay strewn across the street like the carnage of another suicide attack.

It was five thirty in the morning; Jesse should have been sleeping, looking forward to waking up because it was Saturday. Instead, he looked out his window, over all the rooftops and trees, into a grey sky and almost started to cry.

Battles were no longer confined to the hallways and playgrounds of his school. It was beginning to look like the world was one big playground, like every plane was a weapon, and like every student was a reserve waiting to be called into action.

A cold breeze filtered through the window and sent a chill up his spine.

Jesse cringed.

He remembered posing for Elly's camera because she was so impressed with their efforts to make peace. But when they left their houses, they had walked right into another battlefield. Daniel had been surrounded by kids dressed up as soldiers (or was it soldiers dressed up as kids?), and Jesse was considered too ugly to date. Halloween had been more of a trick than a treat. Jesse turned his back on the outside world and crawled back into bed.

Over breakfast, he decided that it was time to bring the fish back to the pond before winter arrived. After clearing his plate from the table, Jesse went into the garage to look for a bucket. He filled it with water and was careful not to spill as he walked through the house and out into the backyard.

Once the fish were caught and safely in the bucket, Jesse grabbed his coat from the closet and put on his shoes. He was about to call out for his father but remembered he was at work, and he wasn't sure his mother would want to come.

Jesse stood at the doorway for a few seconds looking at all the pumpkins and toilet paper and garbage, and he was suddenly too afraid to go outside on his own.

"Mom?" Jesse called out. He'd rather drive with his mom than walk by himself through the carnage.

She stuck her head out from the kitchen and smiled at Jesse.

"What's up, babe?"

"Do you want to come down to the pond with me?"

Surprised, Mary took off her baking mitt and smiled. "Sure, baby. I'd . . .I'd love to!"

Jesse sat at the bottom of the stairs and tried to avoid looking outside the door.

In the van, Jesse was quiet. The clouds in the sky were thick and menacing and Jesse felt like he was suffocating. He felt like his body was imploding, while the rest of the world was exploding. He couldn't make sense of it.

He was thirteen and was beginning to feel as if he was being cheated out of something. Out of what, he wasn't sure.

Maybe it was that couldn't go to a high school dance and have a good time. Maybe it was that he couldn't help Derwin, Daniel, Vanessa, or Salisha. But what worried him the most was the fact that he couldn't seem to help himself. He didn't need to watch the news to see the tragic events taking place in the world. He only needed to wake up into his own life. He looked around but didn't see any cameras, only planes that passed in and out of the thick clouds. Jesse took his eyes off the planes because looking at them no longer amused him.

He retrieved the bucket from the back of the van and led his mother down the path that led to the pond, walking over the very spot he had fallen when he had been hit in the head with either a stick or a stone. He led his mother through the path of dead trees. When they came to the clearing, Jesse walked with the bucket up to the lip of the pond.

His mother didn't know what to do with herself. She stood back and watched her son grow up.

Jesse stood with his back to her and looked across the pond at the crucifixes that stood taller than any rooftop in the neighbourhood. From glanced from one to the other until it felt as if he were shaking his head and saying no to a question that hadn't even been asked. A plane passed through the crosses like a football through the uprights. Jesse didn't like football and didn't care much for planes anymore, so he picked up the bucket and emptied it into the pond.

"See you guys next year," Jesse hoped out loud, but didn't count on it. He was thirteen, and a thirteen-year-old didn't have time for fish.

He walked back to join his mother, who was rifling through the bag.

"Here," she offered. "Chocolate chip. Your favourite."

He took the cookie and sat down on the bucket.

His mother sat down on a rock beside it and put her arm around her son. "Thanks for asking me to come today, Jesse."

Jesse looked at his mother and smiled. "Ma, how long do I have to take Ritalin for?"

The other day he had seen a segment on the news that there was a possible link between depression and people who took Ritalin. Seeing that he was feeling so bad and that he was also taking Ritalin, Jesse figured one way to feel better about things was to get off it.

She looked at Jesse and could only offer half a smile. "I'm . . .I'm not sure, Jesse. I was always under the impression that you would take it until you finished school." She felt a little ashamed at not having given the matter some thought before her little Gift had to bring it up. "Why do you ask, babe? Is something wrong?"

Jesse stood up. He collected few pebbles and tossed them into the water.

"Is there something that you want to talk about, Jesse?"

"Mom, how do you know when you're grown up?"

She walked up behind her baby and wrapped her arms around him and rested her chin on his left shoulder. But Jesse dropped his shoulder and walked away from his mother's embrace. It wasn't time for a hug; it was time for an answer. Jesse waited for one.

Mary stood there looking helpless and worried when Jesse grew flush.

"Can't you just answer a simple question, mom!"

"Jesse, its not a simple question." Mary walked over to him and took his hand, but he pulled his arm away.

"But you're my mom. You're supposed to have all the answers."

It was like a punch in the face. Mary felt helpless. She didn't have an answer and, for the first time in thirteen years, felt as if she was letting her son down.

The sky was a pallet of grey paints, the clouds varying shades of grey, and the inside of Jesse's head—grey. When he could see colour again, he looked into the green of his mother's hopeless eyes and saw fear.

"Jesse, Jesse . . . "

He looked up at his mother and he could see that she was worried. He had done it again. Jesse responded with a lifeless smile and told his mother that he wanted to go home.

On Monday, the halls were ripe with talk about Friday night's Halloween dance.

Daniel wasn't in religion class, so Jesse took his seat and managed to catch up on some of his sleep. He slept all through history, reviewed Freddy Ramirez's computer notes at lunch (because he never heard back from Ryan), and tested himself during science. By the end of the test, he was confident that he had passed his computer midterm. Ryan didn't, because he didn't show up for it. He had taken Jesse's notes for nothing.

When the bell sounded to signal the end of the day, it sounded like an alarm clock to Jesse. He realized that he was still tired, and looked forward to getting home where he could really get some sleep.

On his way through the halls, Jesse saw Ms. Harper walking up the stairs.

"Shit! I almost forgot!" Jesse stopped and threw his bag down onto the floor. He pulled out his Bible and read over his favourite part as he walked up the stairs:

Happy is the one who is
Protected from it,
Who has not been exposed to
Its anger
Who has not been borne of its yoke,
and has no been bound by its

shackles.
For its yoke is a yoke of iron,
And its fetters are fetters of
bronze.
Its death is an evil death,
And Hell is preferable...

"Hey!"

Someone was yelling from the bottom of the stairs.

Jesse closed the Bible and turned around. It was Billy, the jerk from the other day, and he was walking with Wilma from the Halloween party.

She was pointing at Jesse.

"That's the guy!" She laughed and almost fell over in hysterics. Billy was shaking his head. He shrugged his shoulders and pointed at Jesse. "You're fucking joking, right?"

Jesse tightened his grip on the Bible. He turned his back on the two of them and headed for the chapel.

"Why you reading that shit? God can't help you, boy!"

Ms. Harper was at the door. "Do you know that guy, Jesse? I can report him to the office."

"Naw, don't bother. He's just messing around." Jesse took a seat and waited for Ms. Harper to join him.

"Did you get a chance to read the Sirrach passage?"

"Yes, I did. But I don't understand it."

She took a Bible off her desk and opened it. Jesse watched her eyes scan the short sentences, back and forth, until she stopped and looked up at him.

"I think what Sirrach is trying to say—"

"I know what he's trying to say," Jesse interrupted.

"Then what don't you understand?"

"Why aren't people listening? I mean, it's right there in the Bible." Jesse pointed to it, as if to show her just how there it was.

145

Ms. Harper smiled. "It's good to see that at such a young age you see what the Bible has to offer, Jesse. Unfortunately, most kids—and adults too—are too busy looking at themselves to look into the Bible."

Jesse put the Bible down and stood up so as to get a better look at the crucifix that hung above Ms. Harper's desk. He stared at Jesus' punctured rib.

"Miss, did you know Jason Thompson?"

Jesse looked over at her and took her silence for a yes. Without waiting for an answer, he asked her another question that had been on his mind for even longer:

"Why did he kill himself?"

"He was a good kid, Jesse. He had good grades, was good looking, and was very athletic. No one really knows why he did what he did; it was so sudden."

She grabbed a tissue from the box on her desk, patted her eyes, and continued,

"Too many young people make too many bad decisions without ever thinking about what they're doing, Jesse. It's funny—everybody wanted to be like him in some way or another: a good athlete, a good student, popular."

Jesse shrugged his shoulders. "I guess the only person that didn't want to be Jason, was Jason."

He said goodbye and walked back into the halls, hoping that enough time had passed and that Billy had gone home or found someone else to bully. At the end of the hall, Jesse noticed the security camera. He looked up at it wondered just how much it really saw. He heard that they recorded every second of every minute of every school day and that the footage was used as evidence if a problem were to occur.

They had it all wrong.

Having evidence meant that a crime had already been committed, not prevented. Having evidence meant that somewhere there was a victim. The pain had already been inflicted, the suffering already begun. The bodies were already counted; like Samantha finding her brother hanging from the tree in her backyard.

Jesse threw up his hand and wondered who might be watching.

He started walking backwards, away from the camera, daring it to take its eye off of him. Just then, Jesse heard a metal door open and then close, down at the end of the hall. It sounded like a prison-cell door, and that made the hair on the back of his neck stand on end.

Jesse took his eyes off the camera and turned around.

It was Martin and Rudy. They were the last people Jesse needed to see at that moment, so he turned around and headed for another stairwell.

It was too late.

"Hey, look! It's our old friend, acne-boy!"

"Motherfucker just gets uglier and uglier every time we see him!"

Jesse picked up the pace and turned the corner. Thinking it might be better to hide in a classroom, he tried the door of the drama room. It was open.

He walked in and shut the door behind him.

Jesse peeked through the cracks of the door and watched them stalk by.

"Hey, where'd the little fucker go?"

Jesse turned and leaned against the door and tried to catch his breath. He was enveloped in darkness. When his eyes adjusted, he could see that there were five, maybe six people inside. His heart was racing and, if it wasn't for the girl reading on stage, he might have actually heard it. She was sitting on a stool and was reading from a sketchbook that she pressed down with her hands against her thighs. The white pages reflected the light that shone from the spotlight above. She reminded Jesse of an angel.

Jesse listened to her read:

"A world upside down, she doesn't know where to turn,

she feels she has no one, since her love crashed and burned.
She has a boyfriend that loves her, a family that cares,
but no one sees inside her, or grasps the emotions that she bares.
She goes to a place to find peace within her soul,
but it doesn't cure her thoughts, she feels empty and out of control.
Her loved one's screams, brings tears to her eyes
her world seems to crumble, under stone and goodbyes.
Hurt has her soul, and love has her heart.
But fear has her mind, and it's tearing her apart.
Her hand has stopped writing, the lead finally broke,
her tears feel so empty and her thoughts need to soak.
Yearning for understanding, seeps from her sighs,
whispers hide in darkness, as her sanity slowly dies.
She wishes to get away; she wishes someone would see,
she wishes to escape this feeling, she wishes to be free."

It was the most beautiful thing that Jesse had ever heard. Not just the words, but the way she spoke them. No—it wasn't the way she spoke them, but the way she felt them. It was as if each word came straight from her heart. Jesse was mesmerized, his brain paralyzed. Her voice was soft and the words passed through her lips like bubbles being carried away on a soft breeze.

He was enthralled, overwhelmed, and consumed—and didn't realize that he was still clapping after she had walked off the stage and took a seat on the floor.

Jesse embarrassingly set his hands down to his side and turned for the door.

"Hold it, young man!"

The teacher pushed himself up from the floor, straightened out his pants, and walked towards Jesse with his right hand extended.

"I'm Mr. Beckwith," he announced. He swung his hand around like he was pulling back a curtain and added, "This is my poetry group. Would you like to join us?"

"Well, I . . ."

Before he could finish, Mr. Beckwith put his hand on Jesse's shoulder and led him over to the floor in front of the stage. "We don't have much time for introductions, so we'll do that after the last poet takes the stage."

Mr. Beckwith sat down beside Jesse and turned to face the girl that had been reading when Jesse walked into the room. "Natasha, you truly are a poet! Thank you for reading that today. I feel like I was part of something special there. Thank you." Mr. Beckwith rubbed his hands together and looked around at the other members.

"Okay, whose next?"

"I'll go, sir." A boy with long hair got up and took the stage. He cleared his throat and looked at Jesse.

"This poem is called *Tuesday Tragedy.*"

He began reading his poem, but Jesse wasn't listening. He was still listening to Natasha recite her poem. Her words lingered. They were so sweet that he actually felt like he could taste them. Jesse wanted more.

At the end of the boy's poem, Mr. Beckwith walked onto the stage and applauded everyone. "Guys, that was great. You know, I come in here sometimes and I'm tired and I wish I could go home, but every time I listen to you guys read your poems I'm filled with energy. Thank you."

Jesse was feeling the same way. A few minutes ago he was running for his life, but hearing Natasha's poem made him feel good, almost safe.

A knock at the door brought Jesse back to his senses.

One of the girls snickered, "Oh, I wonder who that could be?"

Mr. Beckwith stood up. "Okay. For next week, write a poem about a childhood memory you simply can't forget.

Remember, it's our last gathering before Christmas, so make some magic."

The door opened. A group of teachers, led by Daniel's science teacher, walked into the room. They were wearing sweats and carrying exercise mats.

Jesse didn't like Mr. Grimshaw.

Daniel told him about all the things that Mr. Grimshaw did to his students when they were late or out of uniform or when someone spoke out of turn.

He made one student stand up on his chair for the entire period because he didn't have his uniform sweater, and he told another to take the gum out of her mouth and put it on the end of her nose.

Mr. Beckwith said hello to all the teachers except Mr. Grimshaw, and then walked out of the room.

Jesse followed and joined the others out in the hall.

Jesse introduced himself and shook hands with Michelle, Betty, Mike, Chris, Colynn, Sarah, and Ruby. When Natasha spoke her name, it sounded like a poem.

"Hi. Nice to meet you."

Jesse took her hand. It was as soft as her voice.

Jesse blushed.

"Are you coming babe?" Chris put his arm around Natasha like he was marking his territory and shot Jesse a sharp look, like the one Mr. Grimshaw gave Mr. Beckwith when he walked into the room.

Mr. Beckwith patted Jesse on the back. "Well, Jesse, I hope you can join us next week."

Later that night, Jesse tried to write a poem, but he didn't really know what a poem should look like or sound like. He had written a few poems in grade seven and eight. One of them was about angels and flying and he scored an A+, but he threw it away when Martin told him that only a fag could write a good poem.

Jesse would begin a line and then stop. He scratched out the ones that were particularly bad and tried to build on the ones that were okay.

He couldn't get past the fifth or sixth line, but he wasn't frustrated. There was something in the exercise of writing poetry that made him feel a little less depressed. He recalled what Mr. Beckwith had said about how listening to poems made him feel better, and Jesse surmised that writing them had the same effect.

Jesse thought about things he should write about and tried his hardest when the thoughts invoked a strong emotional response: Elly, love, school, hate, planes, and violence. In the past, when he thought of these things he would grow sad and try to keep himself from crying. But tonight he was thinking about the same things and, for the first time in a long time, he wasn't sad.

For two hours he looked up and down the words on the page. They confirmed how he was feeling and who he was and, even though it made him mad and sad, writing things down gave him an opportunity to examine his life and what was happening in the world in a whole new way: with words. They had a sense of permanence, and Jesse liked the way they made him feel.

Jesse couldn't believe it. He actually thanked God for making him afraid that afternoon.

When he thought about it, he found out about Cadets because he was trying to get away from Martin and Rudy, and now he had discovered poetry because of them as well.

Maybe being afraid wasn't such a bad thing after all.

"She wishes to escape this feeling, she wishes to be free."

It was like looking at himself without having to look in a mirror. He thought about Natasha and Mr. Beckwith and figured that they were both afraid of something.

"He wishes to escape this feeling, he wishes to be free."

All of a sudden, Jesse felt a little less lonely.

Chapter Thirteen

Jesse couldn't wait for the day to end. It was Friday, December 17 and it was the last day before the Christmas holidays started. He needed a break more than ever. He hoped the holidays would afford him some time to relax, unwind, and catch a breath, since so much had happened in such a short period of time.

With all that had been going on his life, Jesse felt the break was a well-deserved one. He jokingly declared December seventeenth "Give Your Kid a Break Day." And because it was "Give Your Kid a Break Day," Jesse let himself catch up on some sleep in most of his classes.

In computer class, all he could do was watch the clock. The seconds passed into what felt like days, and Jesse thought the bell would never ring. He took his eyes off the clock, hoping time would pass quicker if it weren't under such scrutiny.

This was his favourite time of the year because his birthday was two days before Christmas. His parents spoiled him with gifts and praise, and his grandparents gave him money. It was the one thing he could brag about as a kid. But he had stopped bragging when he found out that Ryan's father hadn't bought him a Christmas present in three years.

This year was going to be a quiet Christmas. Jesse's grandfather was ill and wasn't able to deal with the Cullen Christmas chaos.

His mother had eleven brothers and sisters, and Jesse didn't even know some of his cousin's names. They were loud, especially when they drank, and they liked to laugh and drink as they tried to make up for lost time.

Jesse liked the long car rides out east and taking the ferry across to the island. He would stand by the railing and watch the sunlight bounce off the water. His mother told him that when the light shone through the clouds like that, Jesus was coming down from the heavens.

Jesse was looking for Jesus one July evening when his concentration was broken by a plane that flew across Jesus' path. It looked as if it were going straight to heaven. It was the first time Jesse had confused a plane with an angel.

He particularly liked his walks along the beach with his grandfather. As he listened to his grandfather talk about the "good old days," Jesse collected rocks and clams. He wasn't strong enough to pry the clams open, so his grandfather would do it for him. Jesse stood on his tiptoes because his grandfather couldn't bend down far enough. Jesse took the clam out of the shell and let it sit in the palm of his hand.

As he examined the clam, he suddenly felt the urge to squeeze. When he did, a liquid squirted out and shot Jesse in the eye. He was startled for a second, but when his grandfather laughed, Jesse did, too.

"Piss-clams! Piss-clams!" Jesse christened them, and forced another eight clams to piss.

It was a nice place to spend summer and winter holidays. But like so many other things that come with age, things changed. Jesse was older, had passed through a couple more classes, and had been called a few more names. He no longer collected clams and forced them to piss. He had experienced enough pain and torment to know when someone—or something—was feeling pain. Now, Jesse walked the beach but didn't bother with clams, and he wished his grandfather would talk about something else other than the "good ol' days."

"Happy fourteenth birthday, baby!"

Jesse leaned over the cake and blew out the candles, but didn't tell anyone what he had wished for because he really wanted it to come true.

He was spoiled with presents: a mountain bike, a new pair of skates, videogames, three CDs, some clothes, a gift certificate to Playdium, and a model plane. His father was especially proud of the plane because it was the one gift that he had picked out for his son. Jesse didn't think that now was a good time to tell his parents that he was through with planes, so he kissed his father and mother and thanked them for all the gifts.

Later that night, Elly came by for some cake. Jesse hadn't seen her for some time. They talked on the phone a couple of times a week, but she was too busy with schoolwork for walks and talks in the park. Jesse told her about the poetry group and the new poems he had tried to write.

"Speaking of poems, here's your gift!" She handed Jesse his present and could barely contain herself. "Open it!"

Jesse ripped the paper and ran his palm over the surface of his new journal. It was like the one Natasha was reading from when Jesse happened to stumble across the group. He kissed her on the cheek and looked forward to seeing a poem through to the end.

"Elly, it's great!"

Elly pointed to the cover and told Jesse to open it.

The inscription read: *Merry Christmas/Happy Birthday! Thanks for being you. Love Elly –P.S. One of these suckers better be for me!*

That night, after his parents had turned in for the evening, Jesse sat down on the floor in front of the Christmas tree and thought about what to call his new book.

"A Book of Firsts," Jesse said out loud, as if to christen it. He went up to his room and fell asleep and spent the rest of the holidays eating too much junk food, thinking about poems, and looking forward to a new year and the next poetry meeting.

Although many students acted like they couldn't stand school and did whatever they could to get out of it, the truth was that most of them couldn't stand being away from it. They couldn't wait for the holidays to end so that they could meet up with friends, see the girl their father wouldn't let them see, and show off all the things they got for Christmas.

The halls were louder, shoes were shinier, hair was longer or shorter, and cell phones belted out new ring-tones.

Jesse headed to class and couldn't wait to see Daniel. He missed him and was excited to tell him about all the presents he got over the holidays.

But Daniel had a doctor's appointment at 11:00 that morning and signed out after second period. Not wanting to spend lunch alone, Jesse looked for Mr. Beckwith.

It didn't take Jesse very long to spot him walking out of the library. He was trying to balance a stack of books against his chest. His chin was pressed against the top book, but it was obvious that he wasn't going to make it.

Before Mr. Beckwith could make it through the door, three books fell to the floor. A couple of girls stepped over the books and walked into the library. Mr. Beckwith thanked them sarcastically.

Jesse was more cordial. "Hey, Mr. Beckwith! Need a hand?"

He picked up the books and followed Mr. Beckwith upstairs to the English department.

"Okay, here we go!" Mr. Beckwith opened the door and set the books down on the closest desk. He took the books from Jesse and asked him to wait while he put them away.

Jesse felt like a voyeur. Department doors were always closed. Students had access to most rooms in the school, but not the department offices. He had always imagined what it would be like in the staffroom or in a department, and wondered what teachers talked about when the doors were closed. What did they do when students weren't watching? What were they like when they weren't teaching?

The English department was dark. Desks lined the perimeter of the office, and there were computers, cabinets, bookshelves, posters, and postings around the room. In the far corner, in front of the window, a group of teachers sat, cloistered, almost like they were in a huddle.

The only teacher that Jesse recognized was Mr. Grimshaw, Daniel's science teacher. He was sitting in the middle of a group of teachers, telling a story.

" . . . So I figured if she didn't want to do her homework, I'd make her stay after school and clean the desks. I call her my little cleaning lady! I think I'll get her to clean my car next." The other teachers laughed hysterically.

Mr. Beckwith looked over at the group and smirked.

"Hello, *Sam*."

Jesse didn't like the tone of Mr. Grimshaw's voice. Martin and Rudy used the same tone when they pretended to be happy to see Jesse.

"Haven't seen you in a while, man. Where you been?"

Mr. Beckwith walked out of the room, with Jesse right behind him, and shut the door without saying a word to his colleagues. Before the door was closed, Jesse thought he heard the word "loser." He looked around to see if it was anyone in the halls, but realized it had come from inside the department.

"So, Jesse, how were the holidays?"

Jesse picked up his bag and walked with Mr. Beckwith.

"Good. I've been busy writing poems in my new book." He pulled out his sketchbook and handed it to Mr. Beckwith.

"Hey, I got the same one for Christmas. Right on." Mr. Beckwith flipped through the pages and was even more excited to see that Jesse had already filled up a third of the book. "And I love the title, *A Book of Firsts*. Nicely done!"

"I like the title, too, but I don't like the poems."

"Why?" Mr. Beckwith asked as he handed the book back to Jesse.

"I just don't know what a poem is, Sir," Jesse admitted.

Mr. Beckwith stopped walking. "Jesse, a poem is whatever you want it to be. If you thought about, felt about it, and wrote about it, it's a poem."

He made it sound so easy, but Jesse wasn't so sure it was. "I just think there has to be something more to it. I've written all these things, but I don't think any of them truly express how I feel about what I'm writing about."

Mr. Beckwith smiled. "Jesse, there is nothing on the face of the earth that can capture the true sense of what we feel."

"Then what's the point of writing poetry, Sir?"

"The point is that you still have to make an effort to try and understand yourself, Jesse. And poetry is the most sincere way of doing it. It's just you and a pen and a piece of paper, and all you have to do is listen to yourself—no one else. Try not to think too much about it. Poetry isn't about thinking; it's about feeling your way through something until it bleeds through your pen. Whatever comes out on the page is a poem."

Jesse looked down at his book of poetry and felt better about what he had written. He thanked Mr. Beckwith.

"No prob—" The secretarary's voice interrupted him.

"Mr. Beckwith and Mr. Grimshaw, please report to the office."

Mr. Beckwith shrugged his shoulders and threw his hands up in the air. "First day back and I'm already in trouble!" He started down the hall on the way to the office.

Jesse put the book back into his bag and decided to go to class early.

"Hey, Jesse!"

Jesse stopped and turned around.

"I hope you're going to be reading one of those poems soon." Mr. Beckwith said as he headed through the doors.

"I hope so, too, Sir." Jesse watched Mr. Beckwith make his way down the stairs and decided that he would do whatever he had to do to get into Mr. Beckwith's English class next semester.

"Excuse me!"

Jesse hadn't realized that he was blocking the doorway. Mr. Grimshaw walked past him and followed Mr. Beckwith into the office.

When he got home from school, Jesse went straight to his room. He was in the middle of feeling his way through another poem when his mother burst through the front door.

"Jesse! Are you home?" She sounded upset.

"Yeah, Mom. I'm upstairs." Jesse got up from his seat and walked to the top of the stairs. "What's up?"

"Did you forget that I was supposed to pick you up at school today? You have a doctor's appointment at 3:20!"

He had forgotten.

"Can you hurry up, please? And don't forget to bring your Ritalin!"

It may have been -10°C outside, but inside Dr. Sheffield's office, Jesse was sweating. He sat in his seat, rubbing his palms until the friction became unbearable. He was listening to his mother tell the doctor why she was so concerned about her son.

She told Dr. Sheffield about the day down by the pond, how he was spending more and more time alone, and how is moods changed so quickly.

"One moment he's full of life and the next he's so withdrawn. It's not like him."

Jesse hated it when his mother worried about him. Tears were swelling in her eyes as she watched the doctor turn to face Jesse.

"Jesse, there could be a number of different reasons you're feeling this way. I know that these are things that plenty of kids your age go through, but because you're on Ritalin, there is some cause for concern. You may be experiencing the first symptoms of depression."

Jesse looked up at his mother who was covering her mouth with the palm of her hand. She placed her other hand on Jesse's knee.

"Depression? How can a fourteen-year-old child be depressed?"

"Mrs. Cullen, you would be surprised at the number of kids Jesse's age that are depressed. It's no longer an adult sickness."

Dr. Sheffield looked at Jesse, but spoke to his mother. "I recommend that we take Jesse off of the Ritalin and keep a close eye on him. Do you have any important assignments coming up, Jesse?'

"Yes! I have exams next week."

"Well, we'll wait to take you off the medication until those are over. You certainly don't want to mess around with your exams."

Dr. Sheffield got up from his seat and shook Jesse's hand. "Listen, Mrs. Cullen. Jesse will be fine. Just keep an eye on him and let me now if anything changes."

Jesse gathered his things and followed his mother out into the waiting room, where he recognized a boy from his science class rubbing his hands and looking just as nervous as Jesse had been a few minutes ago. Jesse followed his mother out the door, feeling more depressed than ever.

It was first period geography on his first day of second semester, and Jesse spotted an empty desk in the back of the room. He took his seat and looked at all the maps and posters that decorated the wall.

"No Blood for Oil!"

"Peace Also Takes Courage!"

"Fight War—Not Wars!"

When the teacher walked into class and introduced himself, Jesse grabbed his books from his bag and looked forward to learning a thing or two about world peace.

In French class, Daniel was already sitting when Jesse walked in. He had saved Jesse a seat and smiled when he saw him.

"Hey, man! How's it going?" Jesse asked, happy to be in another class with his good friend. They reviewed each other's schedule: They no longer shared the same lunch, but they did have last period gym class together.

Jesse asked Daniel how things were at home.

"As good as can be, I guess," Daniel responded, shrugging his shoulders and reaching into this pocket for his rosary. He told Jesse that his parents' divorce was finalized and that his dad was dating a new woman. Jesse was about to ask Daniel what he thought of her when their teacher walked into class and introduced herself.

"Bonjour class. Je m'appelle Mademoiselle Lanois."

Jesse ate his lunch in the chapel. It may have been a new year and a new semester, but Jesse still wasn't going to take his chances in the cafeteria.

When he was finished picking the peanut butter and bread from his teeth, he picked up his journal to work on a poem but was interrupted by Ms. Harper.

"Hello, Jesse! Exams go well?"

Jesse, slightly annoyed at having been interrupted, closed his book and smiled.

"Not bad."

Ms. Harper sat down beside him and told him about her plans for Easter Mass.

"I know its still a while away, but I'd like to do something special this Easter."

She wanted the mass to be put on by students and asked Jesse if there was anything he would like to contribute to the celebration. He looked over at the statue of Jesus and told her that he could build a cross.

"What a lovely idea! That's great!" She took her pen from her shirt pocket and wrote down Jesse's name. "Why don't you meet with me after school and we can talk about it a little bit more? I'm meeting Jason Thompson's mother for coffee this afternoon."

Jesse looked down at his watch. There were ten minutes before next period began, but Jesse still had something to do.

He hurried off to the nearest washroom and walked into the first available stall. He locked the door behind him, took off his school uniform, and changed into his gym uniform—trying to keep his balance so that he didn't step into the puddle of urine on the floor. He didn't like locker rooms in elementary school, and he had a pretty good idea that he wouldn't like locker rooms in high school either. It was a place where boys tried to be men and where those who stayed boys became victims. Jesse changed into his gym clothes. It was difficult to move with the extra layer of clothing under his uniform, but it was worth it.

After he tied his shoes, Jesse reached for the latch to the door but pulled his hand back when he heard his former-best-friend's voice. The last thing he wanted to do was see Ryan.

Jesse listened to Ryan talk as he ran the water. "Yo! I scored a dime bag from Rasheed this morning. Do you wanna hook up after school and burn a spliff?" Jesse didn't know who Ryan was talking to, but he imagined the person had said yes because Ryan sounded happy.

"Sick! Just give me a few minutes because I'll have to shower after gym class, alright?"

"Damn it," Jesse muttered. Ryan was in his gym class.

Jesse stood in the stall and listened to the silence. He waited a few extra seconds to make sure that the coast was clear, then left the bathroom and headed to Mr. Beckwith's English class.

Jesse took a seat and tried not to interrupt Mr. Beckwith, who was introducing the expectations for the course.

"What I'm hoping for, ladies and gentlemen, is that this class is going to be an experience for us all—myself included." Jesse was surprised to hear Mr. Beckwith speak in such a formal manner. As leader of the poetry group he was more at ease. Sometimes he even swore and begged the members not to tell anyone.

Mr. Beckwith continued, "I hope to learn as much from you as you will from me. I hope this course will teach you a few things about yourselves and answer some of the questions that you may have about the world and the way that it works."

Jesse smiled. Sitting in his new desk, he liked what he was hearing and could see that his assumption about Mr. Beckwith being a good teacher was accurate.

"Jesse, can you give me a hand with the course outline?"

After handing out the outline to the last student, Jesse put the extra copies on Mr. Beckwith's desk, took his seat, and looked forward to hearing more about the class.

"We're going to start with short stories, followed by the novel, some poetry, and if we have time, a media unit. Now, of course, we will also be writing two essays, which I am sure you guys are looking forward to."

The entire class groaned.

"Now, now! I know how you feel about essays—nobody likes writing them. But we're going to try and do a few different things to see if I can change your mind. I think you'll like it."

Mr. Beckwith danced and skipped and did odd things that students giggled over. With the few minutes of class remaining, Mr. Beckwith distributed the textbooks and told the class to copy out some definitions.

When the bell sounded, Jesse felt anxious. He took his time putting his books into his bag and wished grade nine gym wasn't a compulsory credit.

Mr. Beckwith approached Jesse. "Hey, Jesse! So, what do you think so far?"

Jesse dropped his textbook on the floor.

Mr. Beckwith picked it up and handed it back to him.

"Are you alright, Jesse?"

Jesse was flustered. The doctor said he might experience some anxiety when he was taken off the Ritalin. He wasn't sure if it was anxiety he was feeling, but he was nervous about gym class.

"I'm fine, sir." Jesse grabbed his things and headed out the door, hoping that Daniel was still waiting for him.

He wasn't.

The class was already lined up underneath the basketball net by the time Jesse entered the gymnasium. He spotted Daniel immediately and, after quickly scanning the line, was happy to not see Ryan.

Mr. Geddy looked towards Jesse and blew on his whistle. "Let's go gentlemen—you're late!"

Gentlemen? Jesse had thought he was alone, but Ryan overtook him and gave him a shove on the way by. "Hey buddy!"

Jesse jogged over to Daniel and took the spot beside him. He took a peek down at Ryan standing at the other end of the line looking like he'd rather be smoking a joint.

Jesse's favourite class was English.

Geography was fine, and he could tolerate French. Gym was gym, but Mr. Beckwith's class was a blast.

The first story they read was *On the Sidewalk Bleeding*, a short story about a young boy that was killed because he was different, because he wore a jacket with the wrong colours in the wrong part of town.

"Remember: It's important that what we do in this unit, you apply in your own lives. Study your story, look at all the characters, develop character profiles before you pass judgment, and be sure to use your critical thinking skills."

Mr. Beckwith turned his back to the class and proceeded to write on the blackboard. He was about to say something, but was interrupted by the phone.

Mr. Beckwith tossed the chalk onto his desk and walked to the back of the class and answered the phone. "Mr. Beckwith speaking."

Jesse watched and tried to listen in on the conversation.

"You're kidding me? Hold on one sec."

Mr. Beckwith covered the mouthpiece and instructed the class to complete a character profile for one of the characters in the story.

Everyone opened up his or her books except for Jesse. He watched Mr. Beckwith walk out of the class and close the door behind him.

When he came back a few minutes later, Jesse couldn't help but notice that Mr. Beckwith didn't look well- the colour was gone from his face.

"Where was I? Oh yeah—," He bumped into a desk and sent Syed's binder crashing to the floor. Two students in the front of the class were laughing behind their fists as Mr. Beckwith bent down and picked up the binder.

"Sorry, Syed!"

He handed Syed his binder and sat down at his desk.

Jesse watched him reach into his bag and pull out his sketchbook and begin to write something. Jesse was worried, so he did the same.

The sound of the bell startled Jesse, and when he finally lifted his head from the page, he was the only student left in class.

Mr. Beckwith was wiping the boards.

Because he was in no hurry to get to gym class, Jesse walked to the front of the class and approached him. "Sir, are you okay?"

Mr. Beckwith turned around. He was doing his best to keep himself from crying.

"Oh yes, Jesse, I'm fine. Just a little under the weather. Nothing a poem can't fix, right?"

But before Jesse could open his mouth to agree, Mr. Beckwith set down the brush and left the room.

Chapter Fourteen

With a stomach full of bacon and eggs, and a cold slice of last night's leftover pizza, Jesse lay with his head in his mother's lap. She ran her fingers through his hair, and Jesse pressed his head against her fingertips like a cat looking for just a little more love. They watched the news.

The president was set to invade Iraq in what the media dubbed as "the next phase of the war on terror."

A drum roll preceded each news broadcast:

"Good morning. Thank you for joining us. . . ."

"Good afternoon. Thank you for joining us. . . ."

"Good evening. Thank you for joining us. . . ."

Nothing but predictions of when the war would begin, an estimation of causalities, and the approximate costs that were all in the name of making the world a safer place. There were reports of another suicide attack in another city that Jesse had never heard of. He was bored with it all. It all seemed so tragic and pointless, yet there it was on nightly broadcast. Violence in the news, violence in the world, violence in school, and violence in his life.

He wondered how Daniel was coping with his folks, and he hoped that Derwin wasn't still gorging himself on Oreos. Jesse could see him eating them, one after another, as if each cookie was another casualty in an endless war, chewed up and swallowed, fragments caught between the sharp teeth of a hunger that knows no reprieve.

And because no one was paying attention, because he had heard nothing but excuses his whole life, because he got tired of waiting for an adult to come to his rescue (like he thought they were supposed to), Jesse had decided to take matters into his own hands and make a pledge for peace at that Halloween dance.

He had tried to do something about it, but was shot down—became another victim, a casualty. The only peace of mind Jesse could find was in writing poetry.

He used to take a pill; now he wrote words and could see that words were not something to take for granted. They were powerful tools, tools that could kill, tools that could heal. He didn't have to fly a plane to help people. He could help, instead, through poetry. The same way Natasha helped Jesse when he first heard her poem. The same way he was helping himself with poems. Poetry was Jesse's new medicine.

Last night he attempted to quell his anxiety by writing about Mr. Beckwith, but he was thinking and not feeling, so he couldn't write more than a few lines. His mind was a hailstorm of thoughts, trying to figure out what was wrong with his favourite teacher.

Mr. Beckwith was obviously at war with something in his own life. Jesse still had his suspicions about Mr. Grimshaw. He recalled the day he heard the word loser from the other side of the English department door. Who else could it be? What else could it be?

He also looked tired. Not like he was exhausted from work, but as if he was exhausted with life. The enthusiasm that the class fed off and the smile that told them that he loved what he was doing was gone.

He even dismissed the class early on a couple of occasions.

Last week, it was after he was pulled out of class by another teacher with a very serious look on her face. When he came back into the class, he was silent and held a piece of paper. Jesse watched him sit at his desk and read over it with such an intense look on his face. The only time he lifted his eyes from the paper was when he told a student to settle down and read.

"Up to what page, Sir?" Lisa Elder asked.

"I don't know!" Mr. Beckwith snapped back. "Just read!"

Lisa jumped in her seat and opened up to a random page.

Mr. Beckwith suddenly stood up and dismissed the class.

Jesse wanted to help him. It was Mr. Beckwith who introduced him to poetry. Mr. Beckwith was a doctor that prescribed a dose of poetry to cure his pain. Jesse wanted to give something back. He couldn't stand off to the side, like the bystanders stood off to the side when Martin and Rudy pushed Jesse around when they could have stopped it. Like Mr. George volunteering for the war. If there were no one to stand around and watch, then Martin and Rudy wouldn't have had an audience to play up to.

No matter what channel his mother settled on, everything stayed the same. There was nothing new about the news.

"I swear by Jesus, I've seen this exact same headline!" Jesse's father turned the paper so his wife could see the headline.

Bush Set to Invade Iraq.

"I guess the son's doing what the father couldn't finish. That used to be a good thing. What mistakes are you gonna fix for me, boy?" Jesse didn't hear his father's question or his mother's snide response.

"He'll have to live to a hundred and fifty for him to do that, Joe," she joked and nudged her son. "Hey, Jesse?"

"Yeah, a hundred!" He was still thinking about Mr. Beckwith. He was thinking about violence and war and the casualties that continued to mount, and he hoped that his poem was going to be everything he needed it to be.

Jesse closed his eyes until his mother asked him if anything exciting was happening at school.

"I told Ms. Harper that I'd build a cross for the Easter Mass. She wants all the props for the mass to be built by students.

"That's great, baby! You love working with wood."

"Do you think you can pick me up after school tomorrow and bring the wood home with the van?"

"No problem, babe."

The television showed images of soldiers marching, training, cleaning their rifles, and trying not to look scared.

"Ma, can you change the channel please?"

At lunch the next day, Jesse looked for Mr. Beckwith.

Jesse stood at the English department door and perused the teacher's names posted on it. He was happy to see Mr. Beckwith's name. Last night he had a dream that it wasn't there. Jesse knocked.

A teacher opened the door and stuck her head outside, as if trying to keep Jesse from seeing what was going on inside.

"Can I help you?"

"May I speak to Mr. Beckwith, please?" Jesse tried to sneak a peek over her shoulder. The office was empty.

"No, he doesn't work out of this office anymore."

Jesse swallowed something that tasted like fear and stood there as the door closed on his face. He didn't feel like being in the chapel or eating outside on his own, so Jesse headed to the library.

It was his first time back since the September eleventh attacks. Jesse searched for a seat near the back and picked up the pace when he spotted an empty table.

He threw his bag down and went off to look for a book in the poetry section. He wanted to look at some at other poets' work, hoping that he could learn a thing or two about poetry. The poetry section was the smallest section in the library, and it didn't surprise Jesse to see that the military section was at least six times the size of it.

Jesse was almost at the end of the aisle when a familiar cough caught his attention. He looked over and was surprised to see Mr. Beckwith. He was sitting at a table. He was taking sips from a coffee cup and looking around to see if anyone had seen him.

The sign on the front door read "No food or drink in the library."

When he saw Jesse, he put the cup down, put his index finger up to his mouth and winked. He motioned for Jesse to come over and join him.

Jesse took the seat directly across from him.

"I hope it's a good book," Jesse said, looking down at a copy of *The Lord of the Flies.*

"One of the best, Jesse," replied Mr. Beckwith, who smiled a rather unconvincing smile. "I think you guys will like it."

"What's all this, Sir?" Jesse asked. The table was covered with books and papers and the pens that Mr. Beckwith always liked to use. It looked as if he was staying for a while.

"All this? Well, this is me prepping for today's class."

Mr. Beckwith had misunderstood the question. Jesse wanted to know why Mr. Beckwith was working in the library instead of the English department.

"Mr. Beckwith doesn't work out of this office anymore."

Mr. Beckwith picked up a folder and pulled out a transparency sheet. "How are your poems coming along, Jesse?"

Jesse looked across the table. "I'm having a few problems, Sir."

"Well then, perhaps we should have a little chat."

Mr. Beckwith packed up his things. "Let's go for a walk. It's too loud in here to talk about poetry!"

Side by side, they walked through the halls. Mr. Beckwith picked up a pop can and tried to toss it into a recycle bin. He missed. "You know, I can't get over how dirty this school gets."

Jesse walked over and picked up the can and dropped it in the bin.

A few students laughed. "Did you see that kid? Teacher's pet!"

Mr. Beckwith gave the students a stern look. They cowered and went into the cafeteria.

"How's your book coming along, Sir?" Jesse asked. Mr. Beckwith liked to talk about his book a lot in class. It was about a writer from New York.

"Not bad. Same as before, I guess."

Mr. Beckwith stopped walking, like he did in class on so many occasions. When he started talking and began to get worked up about what he was saying, he would stand still and close his eyes as if to reflect on what he was about say. He would speak the first few words with his eyes closed, and then walk around and continue to make his point.

"The problem I'm having is that if you want to tell a story, I think you have to be able to tell your own story first. I mean, how can you write about anything if you can't even write about yourself? That's what makes for the best writing— writing that's been lived. And I'm not quite sure I've lived enough yet to even attempt writing anything, especially not about someone I've never even met."

From what Jesse heard, it sounded as if Mr. Beckwith had lived enough.

He had told the class about his travels to Australia and Mexico City and Paris and Sicily. He disliked England, but brought back pictures of Shakespeare's house to show his classes. He told stories as much as he taught, and it wasn't until he had said that a book was like life—with a beginning, middle, and end—that Jesse realized that Mr. Beckwith was teaching the whole time he was telling stories. Sometimes when he closed his eyes, a few students would roll their eyes, but Jesse would lean back in his chair and wait for him to tell another story.

Mr. Beckwith stopped speaking when he noticed a few students throwing dice against the locker and picking up quarters from the floor.

"Excuse me for a sec, Jesse" Mr. Beckwith walked towards the gamblers, but before he could say anything, they scooped up the dice and the coins and took off towards the parking lot.

Mr. Beckwith came back to Jesse and suggested that they go outside.

They found a picnic table out beyond the football field, and when they were settled Mr. Beckwith asked Jesse about his poem.

"I need to see you read a poem, Jesse. The whole group would love to hear it!"

Jesse took his eyes away from Mr. Beckwith's, feeling a little ashamed, as if he was letting his teacher down.

"Jesse, I've told you. Sometimes writing is not about the end result. The process is something beautiful as well. Writing is like life: if all you do is think about the end, you're not writing or living. Just write and it will take you to the end."

"Maybe I'm too young to understand," Jesse surmised and wasn't quite sure if he was talking about poetry or his life in general.

"It has nothing to do with age, Jesse."

"What do you mean, Sir?"

"Jesse, the one thing I find the older I get is that age doesn't matter. I sometimes think that you students are more mature than most adults. We ask you kids to act like us, but we spend our whole lives acting like you."

Mr. Beckwith's opened his eyes and looked over at the school. "The world can be a tough place for people. Just look at the news, read a paper, watch a movie, read a book. Where are all the happy books? Jesse, when we read *Lord of the Flies*, I want you to pay close attention to what's happening in it. It really is an important book."

Jesse looked forward to reading it.

"Jesse, do you think you can give me a few minutes?"

"Sure." Jesse got up from the table and headed towards the school. Before he got too far, Mr. Beckwith shouted out to him, "Hey, I still want to hear you read one of your poems though. I'm looking forward to it. "

Jesse walked back into the school, where the same students were throwing the same dice. He turned and stood at the door and took another look at Mr. Beckwith.

Jesse hoped that he was alright.

"Hey, are you like some sort of doorstop or something?"

"Get the fuck out of the way, man!"

Jesse arrived for English at the bell.

Mr. Beckwith was in a much more serious mood than he was at lunch. He walked through the aisles and tossed a novel on each student's desk. "I'm sending a sheet of paper around, and would like for you to record the number of your book beside your name, please!"

Mr. Beckwith walked up to the front of the class. He cleared his throat and began his lesson: "Can anyone tell me what it means to be an adult?"

"What do you mean, Sir?"

"What I mean is, what makes an adult not a child, or a teen, or even a young-adult? What makes a person grown up?"

He could see the looks on their faces. They were confused. Mr. Beckwith could see that he was making his point.

"I see a lot of confused looks out there. That's good. Because this book is going to show us that there really isn't much of a difference between children and adults."

The girl in front of Jesse turned and passed him the sign up sheet. Jesse took it from her and opened up his novel.

He perused all the names, stretching back as far as 1994, when his eyes came across a name that seemed to follow him around no matter where he went: Jason Thompson. Jesse put up his hand and asked Mr. Beckwith if he could have another book.

After Mr. Beckwith introduced the novel, he was ready to take some questions.

"Sir, are there no girls on the island?" the girl in front of Jesse asked and giggled.

"No, Stephanie, only boys." The girls in the class felt cheated, and so did a few of the boys. "There are no girls. But I don't want you to look at the book this way. I want you to see all of humanity on the island."

"But, Sir, you said that there were no adults on the island either."

"That's right, Adam. There are no adults. But the boys on the island do a good job of acting like them. Imagine what a world with no adults would be like!"

Students shouted their approval.

Mr. Beckwith settled them down.

"Sir, are we gonna watch the movie?"

"Sir, can I have another book? This one's dirty."

Mr. Beckwith rolled his eyes and dismissed the class at the bell.

Jesse was in no particular hurry to get to gym class. He had forgotten to put his gym uniform on at lunch. He walked up to the front of the class and put his books on top of Mr. Beckwith's desk and helped clean the board.

"You're getting good at this, Jesse! Maybe I should hire you as my blackboard assistant."

Jesse entertained the idea. "Sir, you could use a blackboard assistant." Mr. Beckwith liked writing on the board—so much so that by the end of most classes, he was covered in chalk. Jesse could barely read his writing, but Mr. Beckwith wrote words down and often circled them with chalk because he thought they were that important.

Young adult, war, violence.

Jesse wiped the words off the board and wished it were that easy to do away with all the bad words that were spoken against him over the years.

When the board was clean, Mr. Beckwith slapped his hands together and sent a cloud of dust into the air. "Thanks for your help, Jesse."

"No problem, Sir." Jesse picked up his things from Mr. Beckwith's desk and walked with him out into the hall.

"Jesse, I just wanted—"

"*Mr. Beckwith, please report to the office.*"

"I'm sorry, but I've got to go!"

Jesse watched Mr. Beckwith walk down the halls. He could have sworn he heard Mr. Beckwith say 'fuck'.

On his way to gym class, Jesse couldn't stop thinking about what Mr. Beckwith had said at lunch, about adults playing at being children, and wondered how much of it had to do with what was happening to him. Jesse tried to fit the clues together: the library, the class cancellations, the mood swings. Jesse was thinking about adults as he stood off to the side of the hall and watched two girls yelling at one another, pushing one another, and calling each other names. The louder they got, the bigger the audience. People wanted to see a fight. Jesse saw Ryan trying to jump over the shoulders of those in front of him. Jesse looked around and didn't see any teachers. He immediately thought of an island with no adults and couldn't wait to read the book, but first he had to get to gym class.

The floor hockey game was tied at three. Jesse was serving a forty-five second penalty for tripping. Daniel scored two goals and was difficult to stop. Jesse had no idea that he was that good in floor hockey.

Mr. Geddy was yelling and sometimes cheering. When activities turned into games and challenges and duels, when they became a matter of pride, Mr. Geddy was more of a coach than a teacher.

"Move it, move it!"

"Keep your sticks down!"

"I said keep your stick down, Heffernan!"

There were only a couple of minutes left in the game. Jesse's penalty was over. Daniel had the ball and was working his way up the wing.

Jesse shouted for a pass and Daniel put it right onto his stick.

"One minute left, gentlemen!"

Three defensive players swarmed Jesse. He snaked his way out of the crowd and passed the ball to Daniel, who had to turn around and reach for it.

When the ball left his stick, Jesse followed it with his eyes, hoping to place it by will. When the ball found Daniel's stick, Daniel turned to the net but met Ryan's shoulder and fell to the ground. He knocked him down so hard that his head hit the ground before the rest of his body had a chance to.

"Hey, that wasn't fair!" Jesse yelled as he ran and stood over his friend who was knocked down by his former friend. Jesse looked up at Ryan and hated him more than he ever head—even more than the time Ryan stole his Spiderman comic.

"I didn't mean it, man!" Ryan protested, turning his back on Daniel and accepting high-fives from his teammates.

Mr. Geddy ran up to Daniel and yelled for everyone to back off.

He was bleeding from the mouth, and a tooth was on the floor when it shouldn't have been. It reminded Jesse of the Jack-o'-lanterns the day after Halloween.

"That was the sickest hit I ever saw, man!"

"Yo, did you hear his head hit the ground?"

"Dude won't be biting his nails for a long time, yo!"

"Osama bin Laden my ass!"

"You should get an award for that, man!"

Daniel struggled to his feet. Jesse put his arm around his waist and Daniel's arm around his shoulders and carried him into the nurse's office.

On his way out of the office, Jesse spotted the two girls that were fighting in the halls—one had a black eye, and the other was holding onto her wrist for dear life.

When he walked past the phys-ed department, he could hear Mr. Geddy talking about the hit. Only he wasn't complaining about it—he was bragging about it. "It was the best open floor hit I've ever seen!"

When the final bell rang, Jesse couldn't wait to get out of the school. He met his mother out back, where she was waiting to help Jesse load up the wood for his cross.

After they unloaded the wood in the garage, Jesse didn't want to do anything but read *Lord of the Flies*. He sat down at the edge of his bed, opened up his bag and pulled out all of his books. There was something unfamiliar about his copy. It looked cleaner, and there was a piece of paper sticking out of it. Jesse opened the cover and instead of a student's name, it read *"Teacher's Copy."* It was Mr. Beckwith's book. Jesse figured he had taken it after he helped clean the blackboard after class. He took the piece of paper from between the pages, opened the folds, and read it.

To all parties concerned:

On March 4, 2002, I witnessed an unfortunate incident involving Sam Beckwith and Fred Grimshaw at St. Elizabeth's Secondary School.

Mr. Beckwith had just walked into the staffroom and had taken a seat at the end of the table. He was eating his lunch when Mr. Grimshaw approached him. The two appeared to be having a civil conversation until Mr. Beckwith began to raise his voice. It was clear that he was very agitated, and he yelled, "You're messing around with the wrong person, Fred!" After that, Mr. Beckwith stood up and began clearing his spot.

As the argument continued, Fred Grimshaw stated, "This wouldn't be happening if you were a team player."

Mr. Beckwith approached Mr. Grimshaw and responded, "This wouldn't be happening if you weren't such a fucking bully. You're not in grade six anymore, Fred! You're supposed to be a goddamn teacher."

As Mr. Beckwith was leaving, Mr. Grimshaw suggested that Mr. Beckwith find a new place of employment.

This unfortunate altercation has affected and shaken the teachers who witnessed this incident.

Mr. Sheppard
Religion Department

CHAPTER FIFTEEN

When he woke, Jesse entertained the thought that the piece of paper he held against his chest was not the same piece of paper that he dreamt about last night. But he was old enough—mature enough—to know that it wasn't a dream. This was another nightmare that he was waking up to.

Jesse held up the letter, the top of which fell over as if it were out of breath, out of life. The folds stretched across the surface of the page like scars on flesh. Jesse figured that Mr. Beckwith had read it a lot, and could have said the same thing about himself this morning.

He thought about the time that Mr. Grimshaw and Mr. Beckwith didn't acknowledge one another in the drama room; he thought about the time outside the English department door when he thought he heard the word loser.

Jesse wished that his gut feeling had been just a feeling.

He tried to digest the contents of the letter and the images that came to his mind as he read over it.

"You're messing around with the wrong person, Fred!"

He saw Mr. Beckwith stand up defiantly.

"This wouldn't be happening if you were a team player!"

He pictured a smirk on Mr. Grimshaw's face, as if the point he was making wasn't the point of his objective at all.

"This wouldn't be happening if you weren't such a bully!"
Jesse heard the word bully come out Mr. Beckwith's mouth like a bullet.

A bully? How could a teacher be a bully?

Mr. Beckwith didn't mix words. He was good at articulating his thoughts. If he called Mr. Grimshaw a bully, then that's what he was. Jesse crumpled up the paper because it could have just as easily belonged to him. But it wasn't his—it belonged to his favourite teacher. He flattened out the creases and hoped that Mr. Beckwith didn't notice.

It was 5:28 a.m., and Jesse wished he could just close his eyes and wake up into the March break. He wished he could close his eyes and wake up from the nightmare that his fourteen years of life had become. But the sun would soon be rising, and another day would begin, and Jesse was at the starting gate all over again.

Jesse remembered Mr. Lima once telling the class, after a student questioned the validity of studying history, "For a person to predict what is going to happen in the future, they must look to the past."

Jesse did: elementary school, toy planes, ADHD, Vanessa Musgrove, Ryan, Elly, Martin and Rudy, sticks and stones, breaking bones, acne, more sticks and stones, graduation, Cadets, Derwin, flying a plane, hurting his leg, Mr. George, high school, September eleventh, suicide bombers, the empty sky, a lost dream, Daniel, Salisha, Jesus, Moses, Osama, a familiar face, martyrs, war, poetry, Mr. Beckwith, Mr. Grimshaw, and the look on Ryan's face after Daniel's head hit the floor.

The sound of Daniel's head on the floor brought Jesse back to the present.

"Is this what I have to look forward to?" Jesse asked himself.

Jesse looked at the letter. "A lifetime of *this*?"
Jesse looked at his past. "A lifetime of *that*?"

He thought about Martin and Rudy echoing the sentiments of the most powerful man on the planet: *"You're either with us or you're against us!"*

"Maybe Ryan was right," Jesse reflected. "Maybe the only way this stuff is going to stop is if I make it stop!"

For what felt like the millionth time in his life, Jesse was tired before his day even began.

"Good morning, my little gift, time for school."

The sound of his mother's voice irritated him. It may as well have been Martin and Rudy at the door shouting, "Good morning, my little faggot, time for school!"

Jesse wanted to be alone. "Can you just close my door, Ma?" Jesse's voice cracked.

"Baby, are you all right?"

"Yes. I'm fine!" Jesse snapped. "Just close the door, please."

The seconds passed like hours. Jesse didn't hear the door close, but he did hear something that sounded like a sob.

In first period class, Jesse ignored Mr. Simpson. He was talking about some country in Africa and a war that never ran out of bullets or machetes.

In his sketchbook, Jesse recorded the names of the victims that would never find their way into a history book or geography quiz.

Salisha. Vanessa. Derwin. Daniel. R— He almost wrote down Ryan's name, but stopped and tried to figure out if he too was a victim of something. Jesse intuition was correct.

—yan.

After Ryan's name, it was only fitting to include Martin's and Rudy's.

Kids that made victims out of other kids had to be victims of something, Jesse figured. Victims of victims. But it wasn't only kids.

"This wouldn't be happening if you were a team player!"

He added Mr. Beckwith's name to the list.

"You're supposed to be a goddamn teacher! Not a bully!"

"Jesse, put that book away and please pay attention."

The thought of not seeing Daniel in class upset Jesse, so he skipped French and headed for the chapel.

It was exactly as Jesse needed it to be—empty and quiet.

He rifled through his bag and took out his copy of *Lord of the Flies*. He opened up to chapter two and was only a few sentences in before he lost track of what was happening and had to go back to chapter one because he wanted to make a fresh start.

It was pointless. There was no such thing as a fresh start. He knew that a fresh start would just be the start of the same old story, with the same old characters, the same old conflicts, the same beginning, and the same end. *The end.*

Jesse closed the novel and buried it in his bag.

His eyes were strained and his muscles were suddenly tense, contracting, as if his whole world was getting smaller because he couldn't eat lunch in the cafeteria or hang out at the front of the school and be the first to see something happen instead of hearing about in the halls or over the announcements.

He thought of Mr. Beckwith in the library, and all of a sudden Jesse's uniform was feeling tight and he felt an urge to rip it off. He got up from the chair and walked over to the Stations of the Cross. He looked at the pictures and read the plates that told the story of the man who died for the sins of humanity:

Jesus is condemned to die; Jesus takes up his cross; Jesus falls the first time; Jesus meets his mother; Jesus is helped by Simon; Veronica wipes the face of Jesus; Jesus falls the second time; Jesus speaks to the women; Jesus falls the third time; Jesus is stripped; Jesus is nailed to the cross; Jesus dies; Jesus is buried.

Jesse stood at the twelfth station and looked at the picture of Jesus dying on the cross, then he looked over at the statute of Jesus standing in the corner of the chapel. Mr. Beckwith once told him that art imitated life. *If Jesus couldn't survive, how am I supposed to?* Jesse didn't have God for a father.

He walked and looked at the story of Jesus in reverse, stopping when he reached the sixth station: Veronica wipes the face of Jesus. There was something in the picture that caught his attention. He leaned in to get a closer look, squinting his left eye to see with his right. When he focused on the image on the shroud, Jesse was aghast to see that it was his own face on the shroud, not the face of Jesus.

Jesse felt faint and almost fell for the first time. He held himself up against the wall and took a deep breath. He leaned back into the picture and looked at the shroud and was happy to see that it was back to the face of Jesus, as it should be.

"Jesse, do you need to speak to me?"

Jesse's heart almost came up through his throat.

It was Ms. Harper. "Why are you crying, Jesse?"

Jesse wiped the tear and looked at it. He didn't realize he was crying. "How could something like that happen?" He looked over at the stations and pointed.

"Jesus suffered for everyone, Jesse, and that's why Easter is so important. We come together to acknowledge Jesus giving up his life for us."

Jesse shook his head. "But Jesus didn't give up his life. God sacrificed his only son. Why would a parent do that?"

"That's a complicated question. God gave us something beautiful, and He took it away from us when he saw how people on earth were living. He used Jesus as an example."

"But, Miss, how many times does a person have to be crucified for the sins of someone else for them to get the point?"

"Too many times, Jesse. Too many times. But when He returns, those people will be punished for their complacency. By the way, how's the cross coming along—have you started building it?"

"Ms. Harper, I started building my cross a long time ago."

"Sorry for being late everyone." Mr. Beckwith walked past Jesse and set his bag down on top of his desk. "Now, lets get straight to work. We've got a lot of work to do before March break."

Mr. Beckwith got the class to settle down and picked up a tattered copy of *Lord of the Flies.* "I've already told you guys that this just might be the most important book some of you will ever read. I want you to watch what takes place on the island, and then go out and watch the world around you. I'm not going to tell you what to think, I just want you to be thinking!"

Mr. Beckwith looked at Jesse and winked.

Jesse's stomach turned. Did Mr. Beckwith know that Jesse had the letter?

Jesse felt ashamed at having read it and wished even more that he hadn't.

"Remember, it's important you read the book with a critical mind. When you come across something that you find interesting, record the passage and bring it to class. And I should warn you: It is expected that you will have the book read by the time you come back from March break."

The class erupted.

"Sir, you expect us to read a book over the holiday?"

"Listen, listen. Sarah, stop talking please! Instead of going to the mall or hanging out at the park, read this book. Besides, I'm afraid you don't really have a choice; the day you come back, you'll write a hundred-question quiz. You will not be allowed to write your essay until I'm satisfied that you have read the book, and the quiz will be the first test of that."

Mr. Beckwith smiled. "Now, this is the only chapter we are going to read in class. Read the novel the same way you read the short stories and you'll be prepared. Open up to chapter one, please." Mr. Beckwith cleared his throat and warned them not to interrupt him.

"Tabitha, put that mirror away and open up your book."

"What page are we on, sir?"

Mr. Beckwith shook his head and cleared his throat and walked around the room as he read from the novel that he hoped would change their lives.

Jesse listened attentively and was immediately drawn to the kids on the island. They were survivors of a plane crash, shot down because of a war waged by adults—none of whom were on the island.

Jesse knew Piggy was headed for trouble the moment he walked out of the jungle and introduced himself to Ralph. He may not have had acne, but Piggy was fat and had glasses and spoke funny; he had some good ideas, but no one would listen to him.

Jesse liked the bit about the conch because his grandfather found one for him while looking for piss clams on the beach. The book reminded Jesse so much of elementary school, where everyone started off as friends before they broke up into teams.

Old friends became either hunters, or victims.

They arrived on the island in full uniform, part of a school community—hands up! Hands up! Wait for the conch! Wait for the bell!

The kid with the mark on his face intrigued Jesse because he seemed to disappear like Vanessa had in grade two, Salisha last semester, and Daniel just the other day. He could relate to the part about waiting to be rescued, and he saw that the island wasn't an island—it was the hallways of school.

Jesse lips moved, but it was Mr. Beckwith's voice he was listening to:

"Then they broke out into the sunlight and for a while they were busy finding and devouring food as they moved down the scar towards the platform and the meeting."

Mr. Beckwith closed his book. He looked at the clock, and was surprised to see how little time was left in the period. He reminded the class that it was important that they keep up with their readings because they would be writing their quiz and their essays when they got back from the break.

"Why do we have to write an essay, Sir?" Ashley Ruddy asked.

"Because you need to be able to structure an argument, and the essay is good for that. Here, let me show you." He wrote the word introduction on the blackboard and circled it.

"Now, when you meet someone, you want to make a good impression. I mean Everard can't walk up to a girl he's interested in with his fingers up his nose and introduce himself, right?"

The class laughed. Everard blushed.

"He may have in the past, but now he's going to learn how to make a good introduction—to get someone's attention—and we're going to do it with words, not loud mufflers or cell phones."

Jesse grinned.

"Now, once you've made your introduction, you need to keep your audience's attention by making a sound argument. Back up everything you say and stick to the point. You do this for the middle paragraphs. And finally, before you leave, before you wrap up, you need to make a strong conclusion. Can anyone tell me why it's important to have a strong conclusion?"

"Because it's the last thing the audience will read?"

"Good, Darvinda. You are absolutely correct!" Mr. Beckwith responded enthusiastically. "Your conclusion needs to be a kick in the butt because it's the last thing your audience will read. You need to go out with a bang. The same thing goes with how you live your life: What will your final statement be?"

Jesse took out his sketchbook and recorded the last question. He thought it would work well in a poem.

What will your final statement be? Jesse didn't have an answer—yet.

The bell ended the period, but it signaled the beginning of an awkward moment for Jesse. He took the letter out of his *Lord of the Flies* book and walked over to Mr. Beckwith. He'd only had the letter for a night, but it had felt like a lifetime. It was only a piece of paper, but it carried so much weight. They were only words, but they told a story that Jesse was getting tired of hearing.

"What's up, Jesse?"

"Sir...I have..."

Jesse took a deep breath and spit out the words as quickly as he could. "Sir, I accidentally took this home with me yesterday." He handed the ragged piece of paper to Mr. Beckwith. Jesse dropped his eyes and apologized.

"For what? I should be the one that's sorry. I'm sorry you had to read this Jesse. Remember how I told you the world was a tough place for kids? Well, it's a tough place for adults as well. Sometimes I wonder what there is for you young people to look forward to."

The only thing Jesse looked forward to was the March break.

Mr. Beckwith put his hand on Jesse's shoulder and smiled. "Looks like I have just as much to learn from this book as you guys do, eh?"

Jesse could only smirk.

"Well, Jesse, I have to get to my next class and so do you. Was there anything else you wanted to talk about?"

"Not really."

Mr. Beckwith smiled. "Then let's get out of here."

Jesse wished he was referring to school instead of just the classroom. He walked out into the hall with Mr. Beckwith, but turned away without saying goodbye. He was almost around the corner when he heard Mr. Beckwith shout his name. Jesse didn't stop, but called out, "I know sir, I know! My poem. Next meeting. I promise!"

Chapter Sixteen

Jesse was surprised that he could hear his parents waking up from across the hall. He had shut his door before he fell asleep. His mother was being stubborn and must have opened it in the middle of the night. It seemed it would take a lot more than a closed door to keep Jesse from growing up.

He could shut all the doors in the world, but he'd still have to go to school and answer to a bell and pass exams and enter another year of high school where he'd have to do it all over again.

And then what? Find a job? Go to college? Be a teacher? Be all grown up, but still have to put up with the same nonsense he was dealing with as a fourteen year old?

He had dreamt of nothing but flying planes and hanging out with angels when he was a kid. His mother told him he'd have to go to school if he wanted to do those things. He had put up with so much—the names, the taunts, the laughs, the smirks—that the very thought of being off the ground was sometimes enough to heal some of the pain that he was feeling while his feet were still on it.

He always knew it was only going to be a matter of time before he got his chance to fly, but he didn't think he'd have to betray a friend to do it. At thirteen, he had realized a dream. But that dream had crashed on September eleventh.

"A child without a dream is nothing but an adult," Mr. Beckwith confessed one day in class as he lamented over the fate of the children on the island.

The only difference was that in real life the battlefield expanded and the casualties mounted. Adults played tag with tanks and rocket launchers, hide-and-seek with night vision goggles, and truth-or-dare with a gun pointed at your head. The world was a big sandbox, a borderless playground where things weren't determined by nationalities or potential—they were determined by strength. Who is the strongest? The weakest? Who has the strength to survive?

The strong survive, the rest perish.

Jesse felt like he was beginning to make sense of all the nonsense.

He opened his eyes and stared up at the empty space that his plastic plane used to occupy. A piece of string was the only evidence that a plane had hung from the ceiling. The string reminded Jesse of Jason Thompson and how his sister Sarah found him hanging from the tree out back.

When he heard his mother's footsteps, Jesse let out a slight moan and turned to face the wall.

"Good morning, my little gift. Time for school!"

"Ma, my stomach hurts. I'm not gonna go to school today." Just to be sure, Jesse pressed even harder, "It's the last day before March break and most kids will be away anyway."

"Okay, stay home, Jes."

Jesse turned around so that he could look at his mother. "Mom?"

"Yes, honey?"

"Can you shut my door please?"

She left without shutting it. She walked downstairs and decided that she'd schedule another doctor's appointment for

Jesse. She stood at the bottom of the stairs and hoped her son was alright and that he wouldn't get up to close his—*Click!*

When he woke, it was 9:30 a.m., and it was the first day of his March break. His parents were at work, but Jesse was at home, away from school and hoping to accomplish a few things over the break.

He rolled over and picked up his sketchbook from the floor.

Instead of writing a poem, Jesse wrote up a list of things he wanted to get done this week. He felt the sudden urge to take control of his life and to put a few things in order. When the list was complete, he got out of bed, got dressed, and went downstairs to call Daniel.

After inviting Daniel over for lunch, Jesse hung up the phone and crossed Daniel's name off his list.

He looked at his watch. He had an hour before Daniel got there, so he fixed himself a snack and turned on the television.

Between bites of his peanut-butter sandwich, Jesse watched a repeat of last night's episode of *Survivor*. The survivors were rowing out into the water to retrieve a package of food that a plane had dropped for them.

Jesse took a sip of his chocolate milk and almost choked when he saw the boxes of pizzas and chocolate bars and cans of pop. The survivors were almost tipping the raft over with their celebratory high-fives and hugs. He wished survival were that easy.

Jesse had enough of reality television because there was nothing real about it. There was no plane to drop a care package for Jesse. There was no commercial break so that he could freshen up, and no million-dollar prize for the last survivor.

While he washed his dishes, he remembered a quote from Shakespeare that Mr. Beckwith had told the class: "All the world is a stage." Jesse was tired of playing the same role and wished he could change his life like he could the channel.

Jesse shut the water when he heard the doorbell ring. He threw the paper towel into the garbage and tried to beat Holly to the door. Jesse looked forward to seeing his good friend.

Before Jesse opened the door, he pulled back the curtain and took a look at Daniel—his head was wrapped in a bandage and he was missing a tooth. Ryan's shoulder had left quite the impression.

Jesse opened the door.

"Trick or treat?"

Jesse smiled. "How about a trick?"

Daniel waved his hand around like he was holding a wand and pointed it up into the sky. Then he snapped his fingers and took a bow.

"What kind of trick was that?"

"I made school disappear for a week!" Daniel took off his shoes and picked up Holly.

"Try making it disappear for good," Jesse demanded. He walked Daniel into the living room and took a seat on the couch.

They ate chips and drank pop, all the things that Jesse's mom wouldn't let him eat if he was really sick. Daniel had brought a few video games and, between cutting off some guy's head with a chainsaw and blowing up another terrorist cell, Jesse told Daniel about everything that was happening at school.

Daniel told Jesse about all the things that were happening at home. "I'm doing alright. The headaches are going away, and I'm getting dentures fitted next week. Imagine that—a fourteen-year-old with dentures!"

Jesse looked over at his friend and was convinced that growing up was just as hard on Daniel as it was on him. Jesse felt a little less alone, but was savvy enough to know that strength in numbers didn't apply when you were counted among the victims.

"Forget about dentures. How's gym class going?" Daniel asked.

"I haven't been in a couple of days."

The two of them sat in silence, thinking the same thing. Jesse felt nauseous. Vomit worked its way up his throat and cascaded into his mouth. He swallowed the puke and changed the subject, because the last thing he wanted to talk about was gym class.

"Hey, I almost forgot! Come to the garage. I'll show you the cross that I'm building for Easter Mass."

Daniel put his controller down and followed Jesse.

The two-by-six planks had been measured and cut. The base of the crucifix stood six feet tall, and Jesse had yet to attach the arm pieces.

He turned around and walked backwards until his back was up against the base. "My father's going to help me with the crossbar next week." He lifted up his arms and laughed. "The only person that could be crucified on this is somebody with no arms!"

Daniel laughed and then winced at a sharp pain in his cheek.

Jesse was looking for the measuring tape when he heard Daniel clear his throat.

Jesse hated it whenever someone cleared their throat before saying something. Elly did it when she told Jesse she would be going to another school, Ryan did it when he showed Jesse the knife, and Mr. Grimshaw did it when Mr. Beckwith walked into the English department.

"Jesse, there's something I need to tell you."

"I already know that," Jesse spit back under his breath. He turned around and tried to pretend like he didn't know what was coming. "Yeah, what?"

"Jesse, I'm gonna go live with my dad."

Another one, Jesse lamented. *Another friend gone.*

"Why?" he asked, but all he had to do was look at Daniel for the answer.

"Look at me, Jesse! I look like a frikkin' monster. It really freaked out my mom, and she thinks that my dad will help toughen me up."

Jesse wanted to plead with him, tell him that the last thing the world needed was another toughened-up child. There was enough time for toughening up when they became adults. But he stood there, trying to keep a brave face on because it wouldn't have been very grown up of him to cry. "I guess the coalition has been dissolved, eh?"

"Yeah, but at least we tried."

"Yeah . . . At least we tried."

They walked back into the house and Jesse told Daniel that he had a few things to do this afternoon. He helped Daniel pack up his things and walked him to the door.

"I'm leaving next Thursday, but I'll pass by before I leave."

Jesse smiled, opened the door for Daniel, and closed it without saying goodbye. He walked back into the living room and saw that Daniel had forgotten one of his games. He thought about chasing after him, but instead opened his sketchbook and drew another line through Daniel's name.

After a short nap, Jesse started on his room.

He needed to clean a few things up, throw a few things out, and try to lighten his load just a bit. The first thing he did was strip the collage of photos off the mirror. He figured that if he was going to move ahead and take control over his own life, he certainly couldn't have pictures of his past reminding him of who he was and who he no longer wanted to be—the boy in the picture with the smile that everyone liked. He tossed the photos into a box under his desk. He picked up the mirror and carried it down into the basement. As he walked down the stairs, he couldn't help but sneak a peek at his reflection, and what he saw startled him.

He couldn't believe how tired he looked. He had dark circles under his eyes, and his dark roots were taking over his blond highlights. Jesse looked over his face and could see that the stone in his earring was missing, but his acne wasn't. Jesse thought about taking the mirror outside and smashing it to bits, but he didn't think he could afford another seven years of bad luck. Instead, he set the mirror above the sink in the laundry room so that his beautiful mother could look at herself when she washing clothes.

Jesse cleaned until it was Monday, the first official day of March break.

When he awoke that morning, the first thing he did was look for his sketchbook. He had mistakenly packed it into a box. When he found it, he pulled the pen out of his pocket and scratched off the second item on his list: *Clean up.*

Jesse liked the feeling of being meticulous, of being able to plan something and see it through to the end. His list was long, his tasks many, but he was certainly off to a good start.

Jesse looked at the third item on his list and called Elly.

They hadn't seen each in a couple of weeks. She was swamped with homework and Jesse was too busy trying to write a poem and figure out a few things about life. Typically he'd be figuring these things out with Elly, but, like everyone else in his life, she too gave the impression that she was disappearing from it.

It was cold, and the park was empty as Jesse pushed Elly on the swing.

She told Jesse a story about a girl at her school who showed up drunk and passed out in the middle of her presentation. "And you know what she said when she got back from her suspension? She said that all great artists got drunk. If the school wanted her to be great, than she had to drink a great deal! Can you believe that, man?"

It didn't surprise Jesse. He had heard similar excuses at school. For every late assignment there was an excuse:

"My printer wasn't working."

"My Grandfather died!"

He even overheard a girl in the hall tell Mr. Beckwith that she was pregnant and wouldn't be able to focus on her essay. The next day, Jesse had heard the same girl brag to her friends about how she had fooled Mr. Beckwith and didn't have to write her essay.

Elly turned her head when she didn't feel Jesse's hand on her back. She jumped off the swing and walked over to Jesse, sitting on the same bench where they had smoked their first joint.

"Remember the last time we were on this bench?" Elly asked. She looked at Jesse. He was staring at out at nothing.

"Hey, what's the matter with you?"

"Nothing," he said, and leaned over and looked down at the ground in front of him. "I just want to sit for a bit. That's all."

They sat silently for a few moments until Elly stood up and stretched. "Hey—do you remember Chris Evanston?" she asked.

He did. He was supposed to be Elly's date for the grade-eight grad, but then was too cool to go because he was in high school.

"Well, he called me up the other day and asked me out."

Jesse shrugged his shoulders. "So what?"

"Well, I'm going out with him this weekend. I just wanted to tell you."

Jesse sat there and felt nothing but emptiness. It didn't matter to him whether she went out with Chris Evanston or not.

"Good." Jesse smiled and watched Elly walk over to her purse and pull out a polaroid camera.

"Elly, I don't want a picture taken of me if you don't mind." Jesse minded because if he let her take the picture he would have to force a smile and lie.

"Come on, Jesse! For old time's sake!"

He wished it was for old time's sake—for the times that they sat together on a couch and laughed until their popsicles melted. He wished he could go back to the days they ran around the park together or lay on Elly's bed and listened to the radio, back to when things were easy, when a boy could be a friend with a girl, and war was only a game they played out in the backyard. No picture could bring those days back. Photos may be able to capture a moment, but they couldn't arrest time.

"Do it for me!"

He looked over at her. The camera was already pointed at him and she was eager to take a picture.

"Smile like it's the last picture you'll ever have taken!"

And like every picture Jesse had taken, he lied about how he was feeling and smiled.

Click!

"See! That wasn't so bad, was it?"

They waited in silence for the picture to develop.

Once it was ready, she looked at it and handed it to Jesse. "You look great!"

Jesse took the picture from her and put it into his pocket without looking at it.

He was thinking of Chris Evanston and Ross and Rachel and vowed to never watch another episode of *Friends* because he didn't want to be reminded of what was disappearing from his life. When he got home, he went straight up to his room, opened up his sketchbook, and crossed Elly's name from his list.

Jesse was in his bedroom working on his poem when his mother got home from work. "Honey, I picked up something for dinner!" she yelled from the bottom of the stairs.

"Ma, I'm not hungry. I'm going to stay in my room."

"But honey, I've got Pizz—"

She stopped speaking when she heard his door shut.

Jesse put his pen back to paper and was about to write when the knock at his door threw him off. "What?" he yelled.

His mother stuck her head through the door. "Honey, are you alright? I feel like I haven't seen much of you lately."

"I've been busy, Ma. That's all."

She looked around his room. "I can tell!"

She walked in and stood over her little baby. "Jesse, I want you to speak to Dr. Sheffield, so I made an appointment for next week."

Jesse set his pen down and turned in his chair and looked up at his mother.

"Why do I need another appointment?" He didn't need to hear a doctor tell him that he was depressed and that the cause of it was the pain of growing up in a world intent on making adults out of children before their time.

"Because...I'm worried about you, that's all. The doctor said to keep an eye on you hon, and see if anything changes."

"Yeah, Ma. Something is changing. I'm no longer a kid, and you have to stop worrying about me so much!"

"You're spending too much time on your own."

"Ma, you can't worry about me. You always call me your 'little man', your 'little gift', but I'm grown up, Ma. I'm just going through a phase, and so is everyone else my age. Why have so many of you forgotten what it's like to grow up?"

He didn't wait for her to answer. "Ma, I want to get back to writing. Can you just go? Close my door on the way out, please."

Because she wanted her son to be happy and because she wanted to give him everything he wanted, she turned her back to him and walked out of his room without saying another word. Jesse lifted his head from the page when he heard the sound of the door.

Looking at the closed door, he suddenly wished that it were open.

He had completed everything that he had set out to do over the break. He nailed the last nail into his cross on Friday and studied for his *Lord of the Flies* quiz on Sunday. He reviewed his notes and reflected on his favourite quotes, which he had recorded in his sketchbook:

"That littl'un—" gasped Piggy— "him with the mark on his face. I don't see him now. Where is he?"

"This is an island. It's a good island. Until the grown ups come fetch us, we'll have fun."

"If only they could send us something grown up—a sign or something."

"Supposing I get like the others—not caring. What'll become of us?"

"I dunno Ralph—we just go on. That's all. That's what grown ups would do."

Jesse mulled over Piggy's question and didn't have to look far for the answers.

All he had to do was turn on the news, think about Ryan, read the newspaper, go to school, listen to Martin and Rudy, read private letters, read a couple of books, and do well in school. All Jesse had learned at school was just how tough it was to be a student and just how tough it was to be a human being.

What he really needed to learn was how to survive. And for this, he gave the education system a failing grade. Adults were supposed to teach children how to survive. But how could they teach children when it looked as if they hadn't learned a thing themselves?

Confident that he would ace the quiz, Jesse put his book away and worked on his poem. After about an hour, he called it a night and turned off his light. Tomorrow was the first day of a very important week.

Chapter Seventeen

In geography class, Jesse reviewed his English notes while the rest of his classmates watched a video and took notes for a quiz that Mr. Simpson assigned for tomorrow. Jesse couldn't be bothered with climates and storm clouds, and he wasn't going to let a geography quiz get in the way of an English quiz. He understood the world better in English than French, so Jesse studied all throughout French class as well.

When it was time for lunch, Jesse walked through the halls in no particular rush. He looked straight ahead of him, down the deep dark corridors that ran through the school like veins, and Jesse wondered how much blood had been spilled on these floors.

He walked and kept a straight face, paying no mind to the snickering and pointing. The same old routine, day in and day out; Wilma Flintstone gave him the finger, and Martin and Rudy laughed. Jesse ate his sandwich in the chapel and studied for the quiz under the watchful eyes of Jesus.

Jesse needed to do well. It would show Mr. Beckwith that he understood how the world worked, that he understood how adults acted like children and that what happens to one also happens to the other. He didn't want Mr. Beckwith to feel alone in his fight against terror.

At the sound of the bell, Jesse closed his book and headed for English class.

"I hope every one of you had a wonderful break," Mr. Beckwith started, as he walked around the class handing out the quiz. "But now its time to get to business. You have fifty minutes to complete it. There are a hundred questions, so you should try and get through a couple of questions every minute."

"What?" a girl asked.

"Come on, Sir!" a boy protested.

"If you prepared for it the way I told you, it should be a breeze. Don't tell me how little you studied over the break by complaining about the time."

Jesses finished in twenty minutes.

It was easy—too easy. It only confirmed his suspicion that he understood the world all too well. He felt this because his world seemed a part of William Golding's world, a part of Piggy's world, a part of every victim's world. He was a part of that world, because he was a part of this one, a world where adults treat the world as if it's their playground, kicking around all the children and pushing them off to the sidelines, banishing them to some island where they were left to fend for themselves.

Jesse handed in his quiz and prayed he didn't get perfect.

Mr. Beckwith took up the quiz during the last twenty minutes of class. When the final answer to the final question was given, Mr. Beckwith asked the class to pass forward the quizzes.

Jesse was nervous. He sat at his desk and fiddled with his pen and watched Mr. Beckwith record their marks into his record book. He sat and watched his classmates take their quizzes back after their names had been called. Some looked upset, some looked happy.

Mr. Beckwith called his name.

Jesse wiped his sweaty palms along the side of his pant leg and walked up to the front of the class.

Instead of handing Jesse his quiz, Mr. Beckwith stood up and began clapping.

"Class, please give Mr. Cullen a round of applause! He was the only person to get perfect!" Mr. Beckwith handed Jesse the quiz. "You really got this book, eh Jesse?"

"I guess so," Jesse responded sheepishly. "But I'm not sure that's such a good thing."

Jesse told Mr. Geddy that his leg was bothering him and that his doctor told him he should be off it for a few days and to avoid any physical activity.

He didn't like Mr. Geddy. Not just because he liked Ryan's hit on Daniel so much, but because he always pushed students to overcome pain. When it looked like someone wouldn't finish a lap around the track or their wind sprints from one side of the gym to the other, he'd yell things like, "Only the strong survive! Only the strong survive! Move it, let's go!"

One day, Frank Campos passed out from heat exhaustion because he was trying so hard to be strong—because he was trying so hard to survive.

"Alright, Cullen. But I want to see a doctor's note by the end of the week. And don't forget: Only the strong survive!"

He didn't even ask how Daniel was doing.

When he got home from school that afternoon, Jesse opened up his sketchbook and scratched out one of the few remaining things from his list of things to do: *Pass Lord of the Flies quiz.*

He spent the rest of the evening in the garage with his father, finishing up the cross. With the crossbar complete, the cross actually looked inviting—as if it were waiting for a body. Jesse walked up to it and turned around and stretched his arms out to his side and pressed them against the arms of the cross. A perfect fit.

Jesse turned in for the night, but not before he crossed his cross off his to-do list.

The next day at lunch, Jesse grabbed his food from his locker and hurried to the chapel. He wanted to have as much time as possible to rehearse his poem. He wanted to make sure that the words came out the way he intended them to. He wanted to get it just right. It was his chance to take centre stage and, even though the thought of being on stage and in the spotlight frightened him, Jesse looked forward to saying something that had been on his mind for a very long time—especially for Mr. Beckwith. Words would finally bring them together.

Jesse rehearsed his poem as he walked through the halls and, not paying attention to where he was going, he walked straight into somebody's shoulder for the second time since high school began.

By the time Jesse had looked up to see who he had walked into, before he saw the eyes, the ears, and the hair, he saw the smirk.

"Well, look who it is! You should really do something about that acne!" Rudy turned around like he couldn't stand to see the sight of Jesse's face. "Gross, stop looking at me. Acne's contagious isn't it?"

His friends laughed and jumped up and down and banged their fists against the lockers because they thought it was just that funny.

Jesse yawned because, to him, it was just that boring.

Rudy's face grew rigid. He looked at Jesse and snarled, "What are you looking at, fucker?" Jesse turned the other cheek and walked to the chapel. He didn't feel any resentment towards them because he remembered that they were victims as well.

In the chapel, Jesse found Ms. Harper sitting at her desk.

"Hey, Jesse!" She put her pen down and took off her glasses and turned to face him. "What can I do for you?"

"My cross is ready, Miss!"

"Oh, that's lovely, Jesse. I'm really looking forward to the mass. It's going to be a wonderful event. And just think about it: Your cross is going to be centre of attention."

The centre of attention. He used to want it to so badly. He only wished it didn't have to be like this.

She told him to deliver the cross before class tomorrow morning. "We'll have to add a few things to it before the Mass. Will you need some help carrying it through the school, Jesse?"

Jesse didn't think he'd have too much of a problem carrying another burden through the halls of school. "No, it's okay. I can carry it on my own."

Mr. Beckwith must have been in a foul mood because he asked the class to work on another character profile. He sat at his desk and was writing in his sketchbook, the same type of sketchbook Jesse was holding as he looked at his poem on the page and hoped that it could do to Mr. Beckwith what Natasha's poem had done for him.

Jesse read through his poem and convinced himself that it would be good because there was simply no way that it couldn't be. Jesse stared at Mr. Beckwith. He looked much older than when they first met. He had lost weight and had a few patches of grey hair starting to develop. He looked like a young man growing old before his time.

"So, Jesse, you're reading your first poem today?" Michelle asked as soon as he walked into the room.

"I hope so," Jesse responded nervously, looking at his watch. It was 3:15 and Mr. Beckwith was late.

Mike, who was writing something on the blackboard, suggested that maybe they should start without Mr. Beckwith.

"Not a chance!"

Jesse turned around, surprised by the voice, and was relieved to see that it was Mr. Beckwith, who shut the lights and apologized for being late.

"Let's go guys. I need to hear some of your magic more than ever." Mr. Beckwith looked over at Jesse and winked. "Especially yours!"

One by one the young poets took the stage and mesmerized one another with their thoughts, feeling, and words.

Jesse was not only listening to what they were saying, but how they were saying it. They were well orchestrated, well rehearsed, well read, and well performed.

Natasha's voice was delicate and fragile as she still tried to figure things out about her life; Michelle's poem was sexy; and, Betty's poem was good. Chris was still angry at the world, and Mike was still looking for love from a girl that he couldn't have. When Ruby walked off the stage with a tear in her eye, a lump formed in Jesse's throat. The stool was drowning under the spotlight, waiting for him to take a seat and finally take a stand.

"Jesse!"

Jesse jumped at the sound of Mr. Beckwith's voice.

"Your turn."

Jesse stood up. His knee throbbed, his heart was beating, and beads of sweat gathered under his arms. He had given presentations before, but this was the first time he would be presenting a piece that said something about who he was and what he was feeling. It wasn't about some country's GDP and how it ranked against China's. He remembered his religion presentation when he was about to speak about his mother and how a terrorist attack interrupted a lot more than his speech that day.

He was nervous, excited, terrified. This was his chance.

Jesse took the stage and sat on the stool.

As he opened his sketchbook, the light from above rebounded off the page and blinded Jesse momentarily. He cleared his throat a couple of times and looked over at Mr. Beckwith, who sat on the floor with his legs pulled up to his chest.

He smiled at Jesse and nodded his head. It was Jesse's cue.

"This poem is called 'In Full Uniform', and I've been writing it my entire life."

He heard someone mumble approvingly, like they had just tasted something sweet, and Jesse was satisfied that his introduction had worked. It was his conclusion that he was worried about.

Jesse secretly dedicated the poem to Daniel and parted his lips to read his first line and surrendered himself to poetry, but all that could be heard was the sound of a flushing toilet, a choking toilet, like something being regurgitated, thrown up.

Jesse looked out at Mr. Beckwith.

"Oh, you've got to be kidding me! Jesse, I am *so* sorry for that! It's a joke that some of my colleagues like to play on Principal Scully. He hates it when they flush the toilet over the PA system." Mr. Beckwith got up and marched over to the phone. After dialing, he stepped out of the room.

Jesse's felt as if his entire being had been flushed down the toilet. He got up from the stool and walked off the stage.

Mr. Beckwith came back into the room and hung up the phone.

"Hey, Jesse! Where you going? We've still got a few minutes!"

"No, Sir. I think my time is up."

Mr. Beckwith walked up to the stage and looked out at his fellow poets. "You see how some people refuse to grow up," he spit out in disgust. He shook his head and placed his hands on his hips and looked out at his poetry group. He cleared his throat.

Jesse's kissed his teeth. *What now?*

"Now, I know this may not be the best time, but there is something I wanted to tell you today."

Jesse sat with his legs pulled up to his chest and his arms wrapped around his legs, wishing it were his grandmother's quilt instead of his lifeless arms.

"I just wanted you guys to be the first to know that I'll be leaving St. Elizabeth's at the end of the semester."

Jesse's jaw dropped. This time there was no flushing toilet. Natasha and Michelle gasped, and Mike thought he was joking.

"I wish it was a joke, Mike. I can't talk too much about it, but let's just say it's the best thing for me right now."

He looked over at Jesse, who was getting up from the floor.

"Jesse, where are you going?"

Jesse walked out of the drama room and headed for the exit. He heard the toilet flush one last time and a few teachers laughing in the foyer. Jesse didn't think it was so funny and tried to keep himself from crying, knowing that something in him had died forever—just like the day he no longer wanted to fly planes. He cursed Mr. Beckwith and exited the school.

Jesse played with his food throughout dinner. His father was working and his mother sat silently across the table from him, as if she was afraid to say anything because she had said everything she could possibly say.

After dinner, Jesse decided he'd hang out in his room. On his way up the stairs, his mother called out to him, "Honey, come keep me company for a bit!"

"I can't mom. I have stuff to do." The truth was that he had nothing to do. The only thing he had to today had been interrupted by a flushing toilet.

"Please, honey."

Hearing the desperation in her voice, Jesse walked into the living room and sat beside his mother. She put her arm around her little gift and pulled herself closer to him.

"We're dropping off the cross tomorrow, right?" his mother asked as she flipped through the channels.

"You bet."

"At this moment, we have breaking news..."

Jesse opened his eyes and watched and listened.

"We have just learned that eighty-six children have died in a school in Iraq after an American missile missed its target and destroyed a building that was adjacent to the school."

Jesse watched the rescue workers stumble out of the rubble, carrying the broken bodies of the children that had died. Mothers and father screamed in a language that Jesse didn't understand, but didn't really have to. They were grieving—the universal language of all victims.

"The amazing thing is that there doesn't appear to be any teachers amongst the casualties. We're getting reports that they have all been accounted for and are receiving medical treatment at this time."

Jesse couldn't believe what he was hearing. The teachers had left the children to die. He thought about Mr. Beckwith and the bomb that dropped on the school and how no teachers had the courage to stick around and help the children because they were too busy thinking about themselves, too busy flushing toilets and too busy running for their own lives. He lifted himself off the couch and bent over to kiss his mother good night.

"You haven't done that in a while," she said with a smile.

Before turning in for the night, Jesse opened the door to the garage and looked at his cross. Tomorrow they were celebrating the death of Christ, and Jesse's cross was going to be centre of attention. Jesse crawled into bed and cried himself to sleep.

Jesse didn't need to look at his clock to know that it was five thirty in the morning.

All he had to do was open his eyes, get out of bed, and look out his window like he had done on so many previous mornings.

He looked out at the new buildings, the new malls, the new houses, the neighbourhood getting bigger, the weather getting hotter, but nothing really changing. He looked out at the two crucifixes that towered over the community. From one crucifix to the other, from one school to the next, from St. Gregory's Elementary School to St. Elizabeth's Secondary School, back and forth, again and again and again.

It reminded Jesse of Bill Murray in *Groundhog Day*, waking up to the same day over and over. He watched the same cars pull out of the same driveways and head off in the same direction they had each and every time he had stood looking out his window at five thirty in the morning. He knew that his mother would be walking through the door at any moment to wake him up for another day at school. He would have to put on his uniform and go to a school where the same things would happen—just like they had yesterday and the day before yesterday.

He knew that he'd read books that a lot of people read but didn't understand, because if they had, the story would have come to an end—a fitting conclusion.

Jesse heard the door open. The squeak of the hinge reminded him of how old he was feeling. He turned and saw his mother stick her head into his room.

"How's my little Gift this morning?"

"Same as always, Ma. Did you expect something different?" he replied.

"Jesse?"

"I'm sorry, Ma. Yeah, I'm fine. I'll be downstairs in a few minutes."

He picked his uniform up from the floor and put it on. He walked into the washroom and, without looking at himself, washed his face, brushed his teeth, and went downstairs to join his parents.

After breakfast, Jesse opened the garage door as his mother backed the van up the driveway. He took out the back seat and picked up the cross. He dragged the cross to the van, almost falling over a hammer that he forgot to put away.

When they arrived at school, Jesse told his mother to pull up to the side of the building. When she found a parking spot, she put the van in park and went to open her door.

"Ma, I don't need your help. I can do it on my own."

"Are you sure?"

"More than any time in my entire life."

Mary grabbed her son's hand. "I'm so proud of you, baby!"

Jesse was perplexed. "Proud of what?"

"Are you kidding me? Look at you. You've turned into man almost over night. You're doing well in school, volunteering your time to help others. It's just nice to see you all grown up."

Jesse didn't want to be grown up, but he looked at his mother looking as if she needed to see him smile, so he did.

"Mom, I'm sorry for the way I've been lately."

He leaned over the console and kissed her on the cheek.

"That's okay, baby. I know growing up is hard, and we adults tend to forget that. But can we at least keep the door open?"

"Sure, Mom."

Mary pointed over Jesse's shoulder. "Hey, isn't that Ryan?"

Jesse looked out the window. It was.

"No, I don't think so."

"I think it is," Mary protested. "I can't believe how much he's changed."

"You have no idea just how much, Mom."

Jesse opened the door and walked around the van, where he opened the hatch and dragged out the cross and stood it on end so that he could close the door. He banged on the window to let his mother know that he was in the clear. Jesse watched her drive away and waved goodbye.

He took a deep breath and prayed that there weren't going to be a lot of people in the halls and thanked God for his luck when the stairwell was empty.

Jesse dragged the cross to the base of the stairs and set it down and took a deep breath. It was more difficult than he expected. He imagined what it must have been like for Jesus, forced to carry the instrument of his own death as people taunted him and cursed him and spat upon him.

Jesse picked up his cross and walked through the hallway doors.

The halls were empty.

Jesse was in the middle of thanking God again, when he heard a snicker and a laugh. He stopped in his tracks, set down the cross, and turned around to see who it was. A boy he recognized from first semester ran up to Jesse and knelt down before him.

"Hail, King of Acne!" He picked himself up and sprinted back to his circle of friends who were now throwing high-fives like they had just won the lottery.

Jesse turned his back on them and saw Ryan came around the corner. He was walking with a girl and was limping more than usual.

The boy who mocked Jesse was now taking shots at Ryan.

"Hey, isn't Jesus over here your friend?"

Ryan looked over at Jesse and then at the girl beside him, who was pointing and laughing at Jesse with his cross.

"Hey, babe, I forgot something in the library."

"Library? Since when do you go to—"

Ryan grabbed her, turned his back on his former best friend and disappeared around the corner.

"Can you walk on water? Try it! Please try it. That would be the funniest!"

They laughed and applauded. "If you really are the Son of God, do something about that acne for Christ's sake!"

"Hey, leave him alone. Today's his big day. Don't worry about dying, dude—you'll be back in three days anyway!"

"Don't die for me man. Die for yourself!"

Jesse picked up his cross and carried it to the chapel.

Ms. Harper was standing at the door. She looked at her watch. "Thank goodness you're here, Jesse! Did you forget that you were supposed to lead morning prayer?"

He had.

She looked at the cross. "My goodness, Jesse! It really is beautiful."

Jesse set it down in Ms. Harper's office. He walked into the chapel and was surprised at how full it was.

"If you can't lead the prayer today, I can find something really quick."

He looked at all the faces and remembered his poem from yesterday, and he suddenly felt the urge to share something with someone. Jesse was dying to see something through to the end.

"No, I'll do it."

Ms. Harper walked up to the front of the chapel and thanked everyone for being there. "Before we begin, I would just like to thank all of you who have donated your time and prayers so that we could come together as a community to celebrate the death and resurrection of our Lord, Jesus Christ." She pointed over to the statue of Jesus.

Jesse walked up to the lectern.

Jesse waited for Ms. Harper's cue and hoped that there were no flushing toilets this morning. He looked over at the statue of Jesus. How many times did *He* have to die before people got the point?

From where he stood, Jesse could see a commotion taking place in the hall. The same students that were taunting him were now picking on someone else. Jesse cleared his throat and recited the one passage from the Bible that he set to memory after the first time he read it:

"Those who pay heed to slander,
will not find rest
Nor will they settle down in peace.
The blow of a whip raises a
welt, but a blow of the tongue
crushes the bones."

Jesse looked out and saw the boy get pushed up against a locker.

"Many have fallen by the edge of
the sword,
But not as many have fallen
Because of the tongue."
They were pointing fingers and calling him names.
The boy fell to his knees and pleaded.
"Happy is the one who is
Protected from it,
Who has not been exposed to
Its anger."
The bullies cursed and laughed and ran away.
"For its yoke is a yoke of iron,
And its fetters are fetters of
bronze.

Its death is an evil death..."

Jesse saw Mr. Beckwith came around the corner. He was reading something and didn't see the boy, on his knees, picking up his binder and supplies. Jesse imagined a school without Mr. Beckwith and brought the prayer to a close:

"...And Hell is preferable to it."

At the end of first period, Mr. Wright came over the PA system:

"Good morning, St. Elizabeth's! I just want to remind each and every one of you that today is a very special day in our community. Today we celebrate, as a school, the passing of our Lord and Saviour, Jesus Christ. Mass will be held during fourth period today, and I want to remind you that in order for you to partake in the ceremony, you must be in full uniform."

Jesse didn't bother with lunch. He felt like walking—not in any particular direction or for any particular purpose. He walked past the same doors that Moses held for the bullies, he walked past the cafeteria, he walked into the Hall of Heroes and looked up at Jason Thompson's picture and tried to see beyond the smile that must have hidden how he was truly feeling.

Jesse looked at the rest of the display cases and saw pictures of all the graduates, all those who survived high school. Jesse thought about Salisha and Daniel and Derwin, and he wondered if they'd survive high school. He looked at all the names that made up the honour roll and all the pictures with athletes holding trophies, they were part of a team of winners; but there were no pictures of the losers. Jesse looked back at Jason Thompson and couldn't decide if he was a winner or loser.

Jesse remembered what Ryan once told him: "*You can't trust a person that smiles all the time.*" Jesse turned his back on Jason and bumped into Ryan.

"Hey what's up man?" Ryan asked, as if this morning and high school and Daniel's head had never existed.

Jesse tried to walk by him, but Ryan grabbed his sleeve. "I said, what's up?"

Jesse pulled his arm away. "Hey, fuck off! I saw you laughing with them when they were calling me Jesus."

"Jesus, Jesse, it looked funny, man! A student carrying a cross in the halls—if it had been someone else, you might have laughed, too!"

"I wouldn't have laughed. I would have gotten the point!" Jesse turned his back and walked away.

"You're a fucking loser anyway, Jesse. You always were and always will be. If you want to be Jesus so badly, go home and crucify yourself, you fucking loser!"

Jesse stopped in his tracks, turned around, and stared down his former best friend. "If I'm Jesus, that would make you fucking *Judas*."

Jesse didn't bother bringing his books to English class. Mass was scheduled for 12:15, which would give Mr. Beckwith just enough time to take attendance.

Jesse sat at his desk and waited for his name to be called. He didn't bother with a 'here' or a 'present' because he didn't feel like being either. He wished Mr. Beckwith wasn't leaving. He was the only adult Jesse looked up to and admired, the one adult he thought could teach him a thing or two about survival. But the truth was he couldn't even survive his own battle, let alone help Jesse with his.

"*All classes please proceed down to the gymnasium.*"

Mr. Beckwith dismissed the class. "Okay, I'll see you guys down in the gym. Jesse, can you stick around for a sec? I need to talk you about something."

Jesse sat back down and waited for Mr. Beckwith to collect his things.

Mr. Beckwith shut the door and walked over to Jesse. "Jesse, I'm sorry about what happened yesterday. It's just another *Lord of the Flies* moment—adults acting like kids." Jesse heard the toilet flush in his mind and recalled how his hope for sharing his poem went down the drain.

Mr. Beckwith shook his head and sifted through his bag. "Listen, before I forget. You left your sketchbook in the drama room yesterday."

Jesse watched him pull the book out of his bag. Jesse thought about all the late nights writing poems, trying to start and finish one so that she could share it with his friends.

"Did you read any of them, Sir?" Jesse asked and hoped, in a small way, that he had.

"No, but I'd like to sometime."

Jesse looked down at the cover and remembered how good it had looked when he had first opened it. He handed it back to Mr. Beckwith. "You keep it, Sir. I'm not coming to any more poetry groups."

"Oh, Jesse, don't let what happened yesterday discourage you!"

"It has nothing to do with yesterday, Sir." He was lying. It had everything to do with yesterday—and all the yesterdays that came before it.

Mr. Beckwith put his hand on Jesse's shoulder. "I'm sorry to hear this, Jesse. You'll be missed, man."

"You'll be missed, too, Sir."

Jesse turned his back on him, because Mr. Beckwith had done the same to him by deciding to leave the school. "Good luck with your book."

"Hey, aren't you coming to the Mass?"

"No, I'm signing out."

"Well, I guess I'll see you in class then. Thanks for the book, Jesse. I look forward to reading the poems. Maybe there's a story in here for my book, eh?"

"I hope so, Sir. I really hope so."

Jesse managed to avoid the crowd in the halls, but he wasn't as fortunate when he got outside. There was large gathering out front, which was typical when there was mass or an assembly. He put his hands into his pockets and hoped to get home without incident.

It was wishful thinking.

"Hey, loser! I heard that you think you're Jesus! Try walking on water then."

"If you really are the Son of God, save yourself, man. Don't worry about me!"

Jesse heard footsteps and turned around to see Rudy Sinclair reach into his pocket and flick a quarter at Jesse. "Hey, dick-face! Where you off to in such a hurry? Here's a quarter. Go home and fucking kill yourself!"

They laughed. Jesse recalled the dream when he was down by the pond and how the entire school cheered him towards death.

Jesse picked up the quarter and rolled it through his fingers, then threw it back at Rudy. "Keep it! It's on me."

At the lights, Jesse heard Ryan's voice from inside the bus shelter. When their eyes met, Ryan took a drag from his smoke, exhaled, spit, and took a stab at Jesse with his smile. Once across the street, Jesse looked up at the empty cross that stood atop the school and thought about his own cross. He was sorry that he wouldn't get to see it.

Outside his door, Jesse's hands were shaking and he was having trouble placing the key inside the lock. After a few tries, he opened the door and didn't bother taking the keys from the lock. He walked through the hall and walked downstairs into the basement.

He headed directly into the laundry room and tried the light. It was out. "I guess its only fitting," Jesse surmised. He stood in the dark and damp laundry room and began to cry.

"Doesn't *anything* work anymore?"

He looked around the grey laundry room and imagined everyone gathered in the gym, in uniform, part of a community. He thought about Elly, about Derwin eating an Oreo, about Daniel in another city, and about Mr. Beckwith at another school.

His eyes settled on his reflection in the mirror that the collage of photos had been pasted on. He could see the tape marks from the pictures that had been stuck to it for years, and when he looked at his own face, he saw a face forever beyond tears and smiles.

He turned his back on his reflection and rummaged through a box on the floor until he found an extension cord. He ran the cord through the rafter of the ceiling and made a noose.

Jesse stood there and looked at the hanging cord, like the string in his room that used to hold the plane that his mother had bought him because he had a good first day of school.

Jesse envisioned his cross being carried to the front of the congregation at school and hoped that everyone was looking at it the same way that Jesse was looking at the electrical cord.

"*Lamb of God, you take away the sins of the world.*"

He went to the shelf beside the washing machine, grabbed a gallon of paint, and set it right beneath the extension cord. He took a step back and heard the students on the island chanting:

"*Kill the pig, cut her throat, spill her blood!*"

He reached up, grabbed the cord, and gave it a few tugs.

He thought about Martin and Rudy and the president declaring war on a weaker country:

"*You're either with us or against us!*"

Holly was at his feet, barking incessantly. Jesse looked down at her and needed her to be quiet. He was running out of time. He found Holly the toy he had bought her the day he was knocked unconscious on his day off from school. She stopped barking and began squeezing the life out of the plastic clown.

Jesse looked at his watch. "Mass is almost over."

He bent down to pet Holly. "I love you, pooch!" She licked his hand.

Again, he heard the voice of the priest:

"Lord, we thank you for offering us your only son."

Jesse took one last look in the mirror.

"This is how you remind me of what I really I am . . ."

He looked at his face and set his gaze on the acne that never gave him a chance. He now knew that it was never just about the acne. It was about this world and his position in it. It was a world intent on destroying every gift that it was ever given. He turned his back on his reflection, like he had done so many times at five thirty in the morning, and stepped onto the paint can.

He steadied his balance and reached up for the cord. He slipped his head through the noose and tightened it.

"Being able to recognize inappropriate behaviour, and knowing what to do about it, will help you establish yourself as a leader—whether it's with friends, on the sports field, in a classroom, or out in the real world."

Jesse stood there, on top of the paint can, with the cord around his neck. He looked at himself in the mirror and didn't like they way his uniform looked on him. Despite what he'd been told, he didn't feel like he was part of any particular community. He recalled the day he asked his mother whether the people who jumped to their deaths on September eleventh because they didn't want to be burned would still be able to go to heaven.

"It depends on the circumstances that drove the person to kill themselves."

Jesse was tired of burning slowly. He needed to jump and hoped that somebody would get the point of it all. Mr. Beckwith had said that a conclusion had to be a kick in the ass—a lasting impression.

A last impression.

Jesse thought about his father and the days they spent down at the pond. He thought about his mother and how she said that if he wanted to fly with the angels, he had to go to school.

He wondered what school would have been like without Mr. Beckwith.

Jesse thought about himself and how much work growing up was, about how tired he was and how much he hurt, and about how tired he was of crying and tired of slowly dying.

Jesse thought about the world and all the terrible things he would never get to see.

"... and Hell is preferable to it."

He apologized to his father and mother, then stepped off the paint can and watched himself die in the mirror. He finally got the mirror to do something in death that it never did in life: not give a reflection.

Jesse died, in full uniform, at the exact same moment the priest rang the bell to signal the end of Easter Mass.

"Lord, we thank you for offering us your only son."

Students and teachers bowed their heads before Jesse's cross and asked God for forgiveness.

Epilogue

Because he was leaving for another city and wanted to pick up his video games before he left, it was Daniel who found Jesse's body hanging in the laundry room.

He called 911 and sat upstairs on the couch. He bit his nails until his fingers bled. When the paramedics arrived, all he could do was stand up and point.

The paramedics had a difficult time getting to Jesse's body—Holly was lying under Jesse's feet and wouldn't let them near him.

They found the blue plastic clown and convinced her to go fetch.

When inspecting Jesse's body, the coroner saw just how badly he wanted to die. There were no nail marks on his neck, and his knees were only an inch and a half from the ground.

There was blood seeping through his acne and his uniform was covered in it.

When Mary got off the bus, her heart dropped when she saw all the emergency vehicles on her street. She thought Mr. George had another heart attack.

But when she saw the police, firemen, and paramedics walking in and out of her house, she suddenly craved a smoke and ran toward her home. When she found out that it wasn't the old man but her young son that they were tending to, she punched one of the police officers in the face and fell to her knees and blacked out.

When Mary came to, she was surrounded by family and friends trying to keep her calm and relaxed—but she absolutely lost it when she saw the body of her only child being lead out of her home on a gurney. "Please, let me see my little gift before they take him out of our home. *Please!*"

When she saw Jesse, she let out a sound that no mother should ever have to utter.

"My gift! My only child! Why, baby? Why?" She grabbed his school sweater and banged her fist on the logo. A female officer walked up to her, loosened her grip, and led her away from Jesse's corpse.

"Jesus Christ! My son! My son!"

At school the next day, news of Jesse's death spread quickly.

Students ran to the chapel. Some begged for forgiveness, others just wanted to see a picture of the boy that killed himself, hoping that they had nothing to do with it.

Ryan skipped class and never came back to St. Elizabeth.

Ms. Harper stood in the chapel and spoke the same words she had each time there was a tragedy: "God, it is in these trying times that our faith may be called into question. Please watch over the families of all the victims of this terrible disaster, and give us the strength to do our best in helping those most affected by what has happened today."

Mr. Beckwith was preparing for class when a teacher walked in and told him what had happened. He sorted through the papers on his desk and found Jesse's sketchbook. He looked at the title: *A Book of Firsts*. He cried in a way that no poem could express. He walked out of the room, went into the chapel, and wept.

Mr. Beckwith was away from school for a week after Jesse's suicide.

He spent most of the time in silence, searching for answers to questions about Jesse he had even yet to ask himself. He got up from his bed and went to his file cabinet and opened up the top drawer.

It was full of his research material for the book on the New York writer whose name Jesse could never remember. Mr. Beckwith pulled out a folder.

It was marked, *Jesse Cullen.*

He had kept all the newspaper clippings and letters that people had written in response to Jesse's suicide. One headline read, *"They Teased Him to Death."*

Mr. Beckwith looked at the front page of the paper and could tell that Jesse was forcing his smile.

It wasn't the first time he had read articles about teen suicide. It wasn't the first time he had read articles about bullying. It wasn't the first time he had read about a mother hoping that something good could come from her child's death.

He recalled the day that Jesse handed back the letter and the look in his eye when he found out that adults were no better than children.

He flipped through Jesse's sketchbook and read over the title of the poem that Jesse didn't get to read: "In Full Uniform."

He turned the page and saw Jesse's to-do list and the one item he didn't get a chance to tick off: *Fly with the angels.*

Mr. Beckwith picked up his pen and did it for him.

A lump formed in the back of Mr. Beckwith's throat as he read over Mrs. Cullen's plea in the newspaper. *"If my son's death can save one child from being bullied in school, then what happened to him must be told. He was a wonderful child who did not deserve what was done to him."*

Mr. Beckwith closed the paper and looked into Jesse's eyes and smiled.

"I'm sorry you didn't get to read your poem, Jesse."

He remembered how much Jesse liked *Lord of the Flies*, how he scored a hundred percent on the quiz, and how his conclusion was certainly something to remember. He rubbed his hand over Jesse's sketchbook and admired Mrs. Cullen's courage, reciting her last words in the article by heart:

"If Jesse's death can save one child from being bullied in school, then what happened to him must be told."

After too many years of writing a book about someone he could never truly know, Mr. Beckwith finally had his story: Jesse's story. In many ways, Jesse's story was his story. He threw his chair back and sent it crashing into the wall behind him. He picked up Jesse's sketchbook, ran into his office, sat in front of his computer, and typed up the first line of his first novel:

At the ripe old age of thirteen, Gregory Doucette was beginning to feel like an old man.